THE STORY OF DOCTOR DOLITTLE

TOLD BY HUGH LOFTING
ILLUSTRATED BY THE AUTHOR

Note to the reader:
Published in 1920, *The Story of Doctor Dolittle* became the first of a very popular Doctor Dolittle series. The time when Hugh Lofting was writing was very different from the 21st century world in which we now live, and parts of the Eleventh and Twelfth Chapters that refer to skin color could be regarded by some readers today as discriminatory and offensive. In the production of this Kodansha English Library edition, these chapters have been carefully reviewed and slightly rewritten to avoid any misunderstandings.
We would like to express our thanks to Stuart Varnam-Atkin and Judith Elkin for their valuable advice and assistance in making these minor alterations, which we hope have in no way affected the spirit of the book.

Published by Kodansha Ltd., 12-21 Otowa 2-chome,
Bunkyo-ku, Tokyo 112-8001.

Printed in Japan.
ISBN 978-4-06-513326-2

CONTENTS

TO
ALL CHILDREN

CHILDREN IN YEARS AND CHILDREN IN
HEART
I DEDICATE THIS STORY

THE FIRST CHAPTER
PUDDLEBY

ONCE upon a time, many years ago—when our grandfathers were little children—there was a doctor; and his name was Dolittle—John Dolittle, M.D. "M.D." means that he was a proper doctor and knew a whole lot.

He lived in a little town called, Puddleby-on-the-Marsh. All the folks, young and old, knew him well by sight. And whenever he walked down the street in his high hat everyone would say, "There goes the Doctor!—He's a clever man." And the dogs and the children would all run up and follow behind him; and even the crows that lived in the church-tower would caw and nod their heads.

The house he lived in, on the edge of the town, was quite small; but his garden was very

“A little town called Puddleby-on-the-Marsh”

large and had a wide lawn and stone seats and weeping-willows hanging over. His sister, Sarah Dolittle, was housekeeper for him; but the Doctor looked after the garden himself.

He was very fond of animals and kept many kinds of pets. Besides the gold-fish in the pond at the bottom of his garden, he had rabbits in the pantry, white mice in his piano, a squirrel in the linen closet and a hedgehog in the cellar. He had a cow with a calf too, and an old lame horse—twenty-five years of age—and chickens, and pigeons, and two lambs, and many other animals. But his favorite pets were Dab-Dab the duck, Jip the dog, Gub-Gub the baby pig, Polynesia the parrot, and the owl Too-Too.

His sister used to grumble about all these animals and said they made the house untidy. And one day when an old lady with rheumatism came to see the Doctor, she sat on the hedgehog who was sleeping on the sofa and never came to see him any more, but drove every Saturday all the way to Oxenthorpe, another town ten miles off, to see a different doctor.

Then his sister, Sarah Dolittle, came to him and said, "John, how can you expect sick people to come and see you when you keep all these animals in the house? It's a fine doctor would have his parlor full of hedgehogs and mice! That's the fourth personage these animals have driven away. Squire Jenkins and the Parson say they wouldn't come near your house again—no matter how sick they are. We are getting poorer every day. If you go on like this, none of the best people will have you for a doctor."

"But I like the animals better than the 'best people'," said the Doctor.

"You are ridiculous," said his sister, and walked out of the room.

So, as time went on, the Doctor got more and more animals; and the people who came to see him got less and less. Till at last he had no one left—except the Cat's-meat-Man, who didn't mind any kind of animals. But the Cat's-meat-Man wasn't very rich and he only got sick once a year—at Christmas-time, when he used to give the Doctor sixpence for a bottle of medicine.

Sixpence a year wasn't enough to live on—even in those days, long ago; and if the Doctor hadn't had some money saved up in his money-box, noone knows what would have happened.

And he kept on getting still more pets; and of

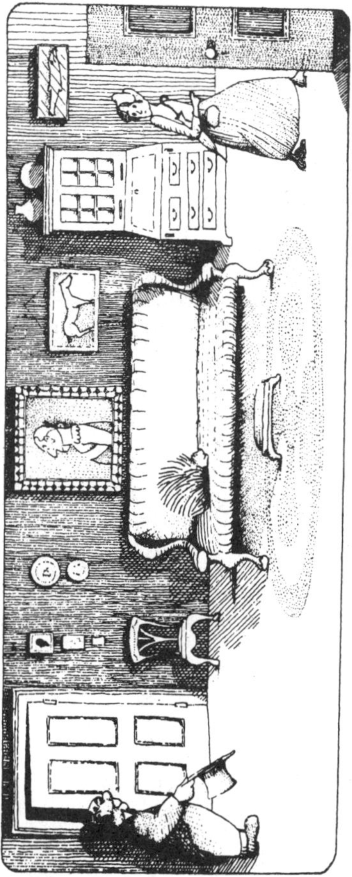

"And she never came to see him any more"

course it cost a lot to feed them. And the money he had saved up grew littler and littler.

Then he sold his piano, and let the mice live in a bureau-drawer. But the money he got for that too began to go, so he sold the brown suit he wore on Sundays and went on becoming poorer and poorer.

And now, when he walked down the street in his high hat, people would say to one another, "There goes John Dolittle, M.D.! There was a time when he was the best known doctor in the West Country—Look at him now—He hasn't any money and his stockings are full of holes!"

But the dogs and the cats and the children still ran up and followed him through the town—the same as they had done when he was rich.

THE SECOND CHAPTER
ANIMAL LANGUAGE

IT happened one day that the Doctor was sitting in his kitchen talking with the Cat's-meat-Man who had come to see him with a stomachache.

"Why don't you give up being a people's doctor, and be an animal-doctor?" asked the Cat's-meat-Man.

The parrot, Polynesia, was sitting in the window looking out at the rain and singing a sailor-song to herself. She stopped singing and started to listen.

"You see, Doctor," the Cat's-meat-Man went on, "you know all about animals—much more than what these here vets do. That book you wrote—about cats, why, it's wonderful! I can't read or write myself—or maybe *I'd* write some books. But my wife, Theodosia, she's a scholar, she is. And she read your book to me. Well, it's wonderful—that's all can be said—wonderful. You might have been a cat yourself. You know the way they think. And listen: you can make a lot of money doctoring animals. Do you know that? You see, I'd send all the old women who had sick cats or dogs to you. And if they didn't get sick fast enough, I could put something in the meat I sell 'em to make 'em sick, see?"

"Oh, no," said the Doctor quickly. "You mustn't do that. That wouldn't be right."

"Oh, I didn't mean real sick," answered the Cat's-meat-Man. "Just a little something to make them droopy-like was what I had reference to. But as you say, maybe it ain't quite fair on the animals. But they'll get sick anyway, because the old women always give 'em too much to eat. And look, all the farmers round about who had lame horses and weak lambs—they'd come. Be an animal-doctor."

When the Cat's-meat-Man had gone the parrot flew off the window on to the Doctor's table and said, "That man's got sense. That's what you ought to do. Be an animal-doctor. Give the silly people up—if they haven't brains enough to see you're the best doctor in the world. Take care of animals instead—*they'll* soon find it out. Be an animal-doctor."

"Oh, there are plenty of animal-doctors," said John Dolittle, putting the flower-pots outside on the window-sill to get the rain.

"Yes, there *are* plenty," said Polynesia. "But none of them are any good at all. Now listen, Doctor, and I'll tell you something. Did you know that animals can talk?"

"I knew that parrots can talk," said the Doctor.

"Oh, we parrots can talk in two languages—people's language and bird-language," said Polynesia proudly. "If I say, 'Polly wants a cracker,' you understand me. But hear this: *Ka-ka oi-ee, fee-fee?*"

"Good Gracious!" cried the Doctor. "What does that mean?"

"That means, 'Is the porridge hot yet?'—in bird-language."

"My! You don't say so!" said the Doctor. "You never talked that way to me before."

"What would have been the good?" said Polynesia, dusting some cracker-crumbs off her left wing. "You wouldn't have understood me if I had."

"Tell me some more," said the Doctor, all excited; and he rushed over to the dresser-drawer and came back with the butcher's book and a pencil. "Now don't go too fast—and I'll write it down. This is interesting—very interesting—something quite new. Give me the Birds' A.B.C. first—slowly now."

So that was the way the Doctor came to know that animals had a language of their own and could talk to one another. And all that afternoon, while it was raining, Polynesia sat on the kitchen table giving him bird words to put down in the book.

At tea-time, when the dog, Jip, came in, the parrot said to the Doctor, "See, *he*'s talking to you."

"Looks to me as though he were scratching his ear," said the Doctor.

"But animals don't always speak with their mouths," said the parrot in a high voice, raising her eyebrows. "They talk with their ears, with their feet, with their tails—with everything. Sometimes they don't *want* to make a noise. Do you see now the way he's twitching up one side of his nose?"

"What's that mean?" asked the Doctor.

"That means, 'Can't you see that it has stopped raining?' " Polynesia answered. "He is asking you a question. Dogs nearly always use their noses for asking questions."

After a while, with the parrot's help, the Doctor got to learn the language of the animals so well that he could talk to them himself and understand everything they said. Then he gave up being a people's doctor altogether.

As soon as the Cat's-meat-Man had told every one that John Dolittle was going to become an animal-doctor, old ladies began to bring him their pet pugs and poodles who had eaten too much cake; and farmers came many miles to show him sick cows and sheep.

One day a plow-horse was brought to him; and the poor thing was terribly glad to find a man who could talk in horse-language.

"You know, Doctor," said the horse, "that vet over the hill knows nothing at all. He has been treating me six weeks now—for spavins. What I need is *spectacles*. I am going blind in one eye. There's no reason why horses shouldn't wear glasses, the same as people. But that stupid man over the hill never even looked at my eyes. He kept on giving me big pills. I tried to tell him;

but he couldn't understand a word of horse-language. What I need is spectacles."

"Of course—of course," said the Doctor. "I'll get you some at once."

"I would like a pair like yours," said the horse—"only green. They'll keep the sun out of my eyes while I'm plowing the Fifty-Acre Field."

"Certainly," said the Doctor. "Green ones you shall have."

"You know, the trouble is, Sir," said the plow-horse as the Doctor opened the front door to let him out—"the trouble is that *anybody* thinks he can doctor animals—just because the animals don't complain. As a matter of fact it takes a much cleverer man to be a really good animal-doctor than it does to be a good people's doctor. My farmer's boy thinks he knows all about horses. I wish you could see him—his face is so fat he looks as though he had no eyes—and he has got as much brain as a potato-bug. He tried to put a mustard-plaster on me last week."

"Where did he put it?" asked the Doctor.

"Oh, he didn't put it anywhere—on me," said the horse. "He only tried to. I kicked him into the duck-pond."

"Well, well!" said the Doctor.

"I'm a pretty quiet creature as a rule," said the horse—"very patient with people—don't make much fuss. But it was bad enough to have that vet giving me the wrong medicine. And when that red-faced booby started to monkey with me, I just couldn't bear it any more."

"Did you hurt the boy much?" asked the Doctor.

"Oh, no," said the horse. "I kicked him in the right place. The vet's looking after him now. When will my glasses be ready?"

"I'll have them for you next week," said the Doctor. "Come in again Tuesday—Good morning!"

"He could see as well as ever"

Then John Dolittle got a fine, big pair of green spectacles; and the plow-horse stopped going blind in one eye and could see as well as ever.

And soon it became a common sight to see farm-animals wearing glasses in the country round Puddleby; and a blind horse was a thing unknown.

And so it was with all the other animals that were brought to him. As soon as they found that he could talk their language, they told him where the pain was and how they felt, and of course it was easy for him to cure them.

Now all these animals went back and told their brothers and friends that there was a doctor in the little house with the big garden who really *was* a doctor. And whenever any creatures got sick—not only horses and cows and dogs—but all the little things of the fields, like harvest-mice and water-voles, badgers and bats, they came at once to his house on the edge of the town, so that his big garden was nearly always crowded with animals trying to get in to see him.

There were so many that came that he had to have special doors made for the different

"They came at once to his house on the edge of the town"

kinds. He wrote "HORSES" over the front door, "COWS" over the side door, and "SHEEP" on the kitchen door. Each kind of animal had a separate door—even the mice had a tiny tunnel made for them into the cellar, where they waited patiently in rows for the Doctor to come round to them.

And so, in a few years' time, every living thing for miles and miles got to know about John Dolittle, M.D. And the birds who flew to other countries in the winter told the animals in foreign lands of the wonderful doctor of Puddleby-on-the-Marsh, who could understand their talk and help them in their troubles. In this way he became famous among the animals—all over the world—better known even than he had been among the folks of the West Country, And he was happy and liked his life very much.

One afternoon when the Doctor was busy writing in a book, Polynesia sat in the window—as she nearly always did—looking out at the leaves blowing about in the garden. Presently she laughed aloud.

"What is it, Polynesia?" asked the Doctor, looking up from his book.

"I was just thinking," said the parrot; and she went on looking at the leaves.

"What were you thinking?"

"I was thinking about people," said Polynesia. "People make me sick. They think they're so wonderful. The world has been going on now for thousands of years, hasn't it? And the only thing in animal-language that *people* have learned to understand is that when a dog wags his tail he means 'I'm glad!'—It's funny, isn't it? You are the very first man to talk like us. Oh, sometimes people annoy me dreadfully—such airs they put on—talking about 'the dumb animals.' *Dumb!*—Huh! Why, I knew a macaw once who could say 'Good morning!' in seven different ways without once opening his mouth. He could talk every language—and Greek. An old professor with a gray beard bought him. But he didn't stay. He said the old man didn't talk Greek right, and he couldn't stand listening to him teach the language wrong. I often wonder what's become of him. That bird knew more geography than people will ever know.—*People*, Golly! I suppose if people ever learn to fly—like any common hedge-sparrow—we shall never hear the end of it!"

"You're a wise old bird," said the Doctor. "How old are you really? I know that parrots and elephants sometimes live to be very, very old."

"I can never be quite sure of my age," said Polynesia. "It's either a hundred and eighty-three or a hundred and eighty-two. But I know that when I first came here from Africa, King Charles was still hiding in the oak-tree—because I saw him. He looked scared to death."

THE THIRD CHAPTER
MORE MONEY TROUBLES

AND soon now the Doctor began to make money again; and his sister, Sarah, bought a new dress and was happy.

Some of the animals who came to see him were so sick that they had to stay at the Doctor's house for a week. And when they were getting better they used to sit in chairs on the lawn.

And often even after they got well, they did not want to go away—they liked the Doctor and his house so much. And he never had the heart to refuse them when they asked if they could stay with him. So in this way he went on getting more and more pets.

Once when he was sitting on his garden wall, smoking a pipe in the evening, an Italian organ-grinder came round with a monkey on a

"They used to sit in chairs on the lawn"

string. The Doctor saw at once that the monkey's collar was too tight and that he was dirty and unhappy. So he took the monkey away from the Italian, gave the man a shilling and told him to go. The organ-grinder got awfully angry and said that he wanted to keep the monkey. But the Doctor told him that if he didn't go away he would punch him on the nose. John Dolittle was a strong man, though he wasn't very tall. So the Italian went away saying rude things and the monkey stayed with Doctor Dolittle and had a good home. The other animals in the house called him "Chee-Chee"—which is a common word in monkey-language, meaning "ginger."

And another time, when the circus came to Puddleby, the crocodile who had a bad toothache escaped at night and came into the Doctor's garden. The Doctor talked to him in crocodile-language and took him into the house and made his tooth better. But when the crocodile saw what a nice house it was—with all the different places for the different kinds of animals—he too wanted to live with the Doctor. He asked couldn't he sleep in the fish-pond at the bottom of the garden, if he promised not to eat the fish. When the circus-men came to take him back he got so wild and savage that he frightened them away. But to every one in the house he was always as gentle as a kitten.

But now the old ladies grew afraid to send their lap-dogs to Doctor Dolittle because of the crocodile; and the farmers wouldn't believe that he would not eat the lambs and sick calves they brought to be cured. So the Doctor went to the crocodile and told him he must go back to his circus. But he wept such big tears, and begged so hard to be allowed to stay, that the Doctor hadn't the heart to turn him out.

So then the Doctor's sister came to him and said, "John, you must send that creature away.

Now the farmers and the old ladies are afraid to send their animals to you—just as we were beginning to be well off again. Now we shall be ruined entirely. This is the last straw. I will no longer be housekeeper for you if you don't send away that alligator."

"It isn't an alligator," said the Doctor—"it's a crocodile."

"I don't care what you call it," said his sister. "It's a nasty thing to find under the bed. I won't have it in the house."

"But he has promised me," the Doctor answered, "that he will not bite any one. He doesn't like the circus; and I haven't the money to send him back to Africa where he comes from. He minds his own business and on the whole is very well behaved. Don't be so fussy."

"I tell you I *will not* have him around," said Sarah. "He eats the linoleum. If you don't send him away this minute I'll—I'll go and get married!"

"All right," said the Doctor, "go and get married. It can't be helped." And he took down his hat and went out into the garden.

So Sarah Dolittle packed up her things and went off; and the Doctor was left all alone with his animal family.

" 'All right,' said the Doctor, 'go and get married' "

And very soon he was poorer than he had ever been before. With all these mouths to fill, and the house to look after, and no one to do the mending, and no money coming in to pay the butcher's bill, things began to look very difficult. But the Doctor didn't worry at all.

"Money is a nuisance," he used to say. "We'd all be much better off if it had never been invented. What does money matter, so long as we are happy?"

But soon the animals themselves began to get worried. And one evening when the Doctor was asleep in his chair before the kitchen-fire they began talking it over among themselves in whispers. And the owl, Too-Too, who was good at arithmetic, figured it out that there was only money enough left to last another week—if they each had one meal a day and no more.

Then the parrot said, "I think we all ought to do the housework ourselves. At least we can do that much. After all, it is for our sakes that the old man finds himself so lonely and so poor."

So it was agreed that the monkey, Chee-Chee, was to do the cooking and mending; the dog was to sweep the floors; the duck was to dust and make the beds; the owl, Too-Too, was to keep the accounts, and the pig was to do the gardening. They made Polynesia, the parrot, housekeeper and laundress, because she was the oldest.

Of course at first they all found their new jobs very hard to do—all except Chee-Chee, who had hands, and could do things like a man. But they soon got used to it; and they used to think it great fun to watch Jip, the dog, sweeping his tail over the floor with a rag tied onto it for a broom. After a little they got to do the work so well that the Doctor said that he had never had

"One evening when the Doctor was asleep in his chair"

his house kept so tidy or so clean before.

In this way things went along all right for a while; but without money they found it very hard.

Then the animals made a vegetable and flower stall outside the garden-gate and sold radishes and roses to the people that passed by along the road.

But still they didn't seem to make enough money to pay all the bills—and still the Doctor wouldn't worry. When the parrot came to him and told him that the fishmonger wouldn't give them any more fish, he said, "Never mind. So long as the hens lay eggs and the cow gives milk we can have omeletes and junket. And there are plenty of vegetables left in the garden. The winter is still a long way off. Don't fuss. That was the trouble with Sarah—she would fuss. I wonder how Sarah's getting on—an excellent woman—in some ways—well, well!"

But the snow came earlier than usual that year; and although the old lame horse hauled in plenty of wood from the forest outside the town, so they could have a big fire in the kitchen, most of the vegetables in the garden were gone, and the rest were covered with snow; and many of the animals were really hungry.

THE FOURTH CHAPTER
A MESSAGE FROM AFRICA

THAT winter was a very cold one. And one night in December, when they were all sitting round the warm fire in the kitchen, and the Doctor was reading aloud to them out of books he had written himself in animal-language, the owl, Too-Too, suddenly said, "Sh! What's that noise outside?"

They all listened; and presently they heard the sound of someone running. Then the door flew open and the monkey, Chee-Chee, ran in, badly out of breath.

"Doctor!" he cried, "I've just had a message from a cousin of mine in Africa. There is a terrible sickness among the monkeys out there. They are all catching it—and they are dying in hundreds. They have heard of you, and beg you to come to Africa to stop the sickness."

"Who brought the message?" asked the Doctor, taking off his spectacles and laying down his book.

"A swallow," said Chee-Chee. "She is outside on the rain-butt."

"Bring her in by the fire," said the Doctor. "She must be perished with the cold. The swallows flew South six weeks ago!"

So the swallow was brought in, all huddled and shivering; and although she was a little afraid at first, she soon got warmed up and sat on the edge of the mantelpiece and began to talk.

When she had finished the Doctor said, "I would gladly go to Africa—especially in this bitter weather. But I'm afraid we haven't money enough to buy the tickets. Get me the money box, Chee-Chee."

So the monkey climbed up and got it off the top shelf of the dresser.

There was nothing in it—not one single penny!

"I felt sure there was twopence left," said the Doctor.

"There *was*," said the owl. "But you spent it on a rattle for that badger's baby when he was teething."

"Did I?" said the Doctor—"dear me, dear me! What a nuisance money is, to be sure! Well, never mind. Perhaps if I go down to the seaside I shall be able to borrow a boat that will take us to Africa. I knew a seaman once who brought his baby to me with measles. Maybe he'll lend us his boat—the baby got well."

" 'I felt sure there was twopence left' "

So early the next morning the Doctor went down to the sea-shore. And when he came back he told the animals it was all right—the sailor was going to lend them the boat.

Then the crocodile and the monkey and the parrot were very glad and began to sing, because they were going back to Africa, their real home. And the Doctor said, "I shall only be able to take you three—with Jip the dog, Dab-Dab the duck, Gub-Gub the pig and the owl, Too-Too. The rest of the animals, like the dormice and the water-voles and the bats, they will have to go back and live in the fields where they were born till we come home again. But as most of them sleep through the winter, they won't mind that—and besides, it wouldn't be good for them to go to Africa."

So then the parrot, who had been on long sea-voyages before, began telling the Doctor all the things he would have to take with him on the ship.

"You must have plenty of pilot-bread," she said—" 'hard tack' they call it. And you must have beef in cans—and an anchor."

"I expect the ship will have its own anchor," said the Doctor.

"Well, make sure," said Polynesia. "Because it's very important. You can't stop if you haven't got an anchor. And you'll need a bell."

"What's that for?" asked the Doctor.

"To tell the time by," said the parrot. "You go and ring it every half-hour and then you know what time it is. And bring a whole lot of rope—it always comes in handy on voyages."

Then they began to wonder where they were going to get the money from to buy all the things they needed.

"Oh, bother it! Money again," cried the Doctor. "Goodness! I shall be glad to get to Africa where we don't have to have any! I'll go and ask the grocer if he will wait for his money till I get back—no, I'll send the sailor to ask him."

So the sailor went to see the grocer. And presently he came back with all the things they wanted.

Then the animals packed up; and after they had turned off the water so the pipes wouldn't freeze, and put up the shutters, they closed the house and gave the key to the old horse who lived in the stable. And when they had seen that there was plenty of hay in the loft to last the horse through the Winter, they carried all their luggage down to the seashore and got on to the boat.

The Cat's-meat-Man was there to see them off; and he brought a large suet-pudding as a present for the Doctor because, he said he had been told, you couldn't get suet-puddings in foreign parts.

As soon as they were on the ship, Gub-Gub, the pig, asked where the beds were, for it was four o'clock in the afternoon and he wanted his nap. So Polynesia took him downstairs into the inside of the ship and showed him the beds, set all on top of one another like bookshelves against a wall.

"Why, that isn't a bed!" cried Gub-Gub. "That's a shelf!"

"Beds are always like that on ships," said the parrot. "It isn't a shelf. Climb up into it and go to sleep. That's what you call 'a bunk.' "

"I don't think I'll go to bed yet," said Gub-Gub. "I'm too excited. I want to go upstairs again and see them start."

"Well, this is your first trip," said Polynesia. "You will get used to the life after a while." And she went back up the stairs of the ship, humming this song to herself,

I've seen the Black Sea and the Red Sea;
  I rounded the Isle of Wight;
I discovered the Yellow River,
  And the Orange too—by night.
Now Greenland drops behind again,

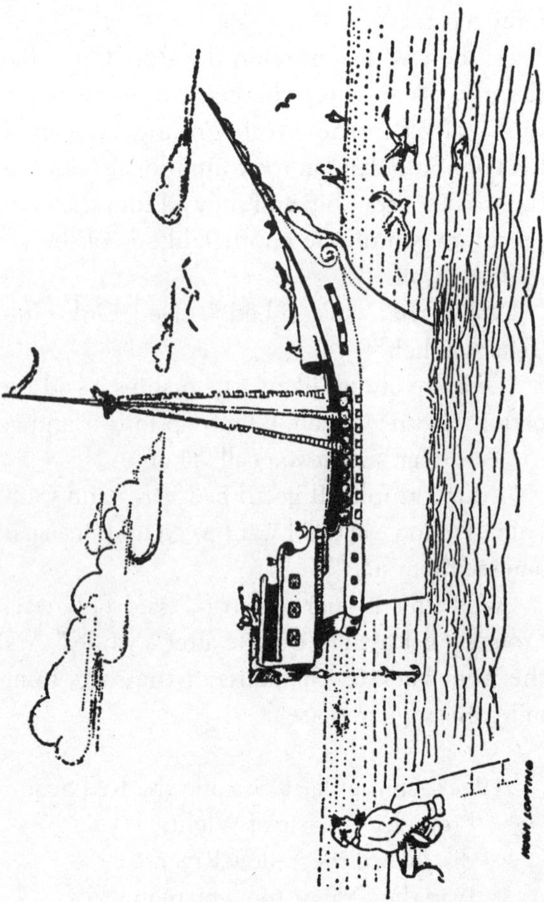

"And the voyage began"

And I sail the ocean Blue.
I'm tired of all these colors, Jane,
So I'm coming back to you.

They were just going to start on their journey, when the Doctor said he would have to go back and ask the sailor the way to Africa.

But the swallow said she had been to that country many times and would show them how to get there.

So the Doctor told Chee-Chee to pull up the anchor and the voyage began.

THE FIFTH CHAPTER

THE GREAT JOURNEY

NOW for six whole weeks they went sailing on and on, over the rolling sea, following the swallow who flew before the ship to show them the way. At night she carried a tiny lantern, so they should not miss her in the dark; and the people on the other ships that passed said that the light must be a shooting star.

As they sailed further and further into the South, it got warmer and warmer. Polynesia, Chee-Chee and the crocodile enjoyed the hot sun no end. They ran about laughing and looking over the side of the ship to see if they could see Africa yet.

But the pig and the dog and the owl, Too-Too, could do nothing in such weather, but sat at the end of the ship in the shade of a big barrel, with their tongues hanging out, drinking lemonade.

Dab-Dab, the duck, used to keep herself cool by jumping into the sea and swimming behind the ship. And every once in a while, when the top of her head got too hot, she would dive under the ship and come up on the other side. In this way, too, she used to catch herrings on Tuesdays and Fridays—when everybody on the boat ate fish to make the beef last longer.

When they got near to the Equator they saw some flying-fishes coming towards them. And the fishes asked the parrot if this was Doctor Dolittle's ship. When she told them it was, they said they were glad, because the monkeys in Africa were getting worried that he would never come. Polynesia asked them how many miles they had yet to go; and the flying-fishes said it was only fifty-five miles now to the coast of Africa.

And another time a whole school of porpoises came dancing through the waves; and they too asked Polynesia if this was the ship of the famous doctor. And when they heard that it was, they asked the parrot if the Doctor wanted anything for his journey.

And Polynesia said, "Yes. We have run short of onions."

"There is an island not far from here," said the porpoises, "where the wild onions grow tall and strong. Keep straight on—we will get some and catch up to you."

So the porpoises dashed away through the sea. And very soon the parrot saw them again, coming up behind, dragging the onions through the waves in big nets made of seaweed.

The next evening, as the sun was going down, the Doctor said, "Get me the telescope, Chee-Chee. Our journey is nearly ended. Very soon we should be able to see the shores of Africa."

And about half an hour later, sure enough, they thought they could see something in front that might be land. But it began to get darker and darker and they couldn't be sure.

Then a great storm came up, with thunder and lightning. The wind howled; the rain came down in torrents; and the waves got so high they splashed right over the boat.

Presently there was a big BANG! The ship stopped and rolled over on its side.

"What's happened?" asked the Doctor, coming up from downstairs.

"I'm not sure," said the parrot; "but I think we're ship-wrecked. Tell the duck to get out and see."

So Dab-Dab dived right down under the waves. And when she came up she said they had struck a rock; there was a big hole in the bottom of the ship; the water was coming in; and they were sinking fast.

"We must have run into Africa," said the Doctor. "Dear me, dear me!—Well—we must all swim to land."

But Chee-Chee and Gub-Gub did not know how to swim.

"Get the rope!" said Polynesia. "I told you it would come in handy. Where's that duck? Come here, Dab-Dab. Take this end of the rope, fly to the shore and tie it on to a palm-tree; and we'll hold the other end on the ship here. Then those that can't swim must climb along the rope till they reach the land. That's what you call a 'life-line.' "

So they all got safely to the shore—some swimming, some flying; and those that climbed along the rope brought the Doctor's trunk and hand-bag with them.

But the ship was no good any more—with the

“ ‘We must have run into Africa’ ”

big hole in the bottom; and presently the rough sea beat it to pieces on the rocks and the timbers floated away.

Then they all took shelter in a nice dry cave they found, high up in the cliffs, till the storm was over.

When the sun came out next morning they went down to the sandy beach to dry themselves.

"Dear old Africa!" sighed Polynesia. "It's good to get back. Just think—it'll be a hundred and sixty-nine years tomorrow since I was here! And it hasn't changed a bit!—Same old palm-trees; same old red earth; same old black ants! There's no place like home!"

And the others noticed she had tears in her eyes—she was so pleased to see her country once again.

Then the Doctor missed his high hat; for it had been blown into the sea during the storm. So Dab-Dab went out to look for it. And presently she saw it, a long way off, floating on the water like a toy-boat.

When she flew down to get it, she found one of the white mice, very frightened, sitting inside it.

"What are you doing here?" asked the duck. "You were told to stay behind in Puddleby."

"I didn't want to be left behind," said the mouse. "I wanted to see what Africa was like—I have relatives there. So I hid in the baggage and was brought on to the ship with the hard-tack. When the ship sank I was terribly frightened—because I cannot swim far. I swam as long as I could, but I soon got all exhausted and thought I was going to sink. And then, just at that moment, the old man's hat came floating by; and I got into it because I did not want to be drowned."

So the duck took up the hat with the mouse in it and brought it to the Doctor on the shore. And they all gathered round to have a look.

"That's what you call a 'stowaway,' " said the parrot.

Presently, when they were looking for a place in the trunk where the white mouse could travel comfortably, the monkey, Chee-Chee, suddenly said, "Sh! I hear footsteps in the jungle!"

They all stopped talking and listened. And soon a black man came down out of the woods and asked them what they were doing there.

"My name is John Dolittle—M.D.," said the Doctor. "I have been asked to come to Africa to cure the monkeys who are sick."

"You must all come before the King," said the man.

"What king?" asked the Doctor, who didn't want to waste any time.

"The King of the Jolliginki," the man answered. "All these lands belong to him; and all strangers must be brought before him. Follow me."

“ ‘I got into it because I did not want to be drowned’ ”

So they gathered up their baggage and went off, following the man through the jungle.

THE SIXTH CHAPTER
POLYNESIA AND THE KING

WHEN they had gone a little way through the thick forest, they came to a wide, clear space; and they saw the King's palace which was made of mud.

This was where the King lived with his Queen, Ermintrude, and their teenage son, Prince Bumpo. The Prince was away playing tennis. But the King and Queen were sitting under an umbrella before the palace door. And Queen Ermintrude was asleep.

When the Doctor had come up to the palace the King asked him his business; and the Doctor told him why he had come to Africa.

"You may not travel through my lands," said the King. "Many years ago a white man came to these shores; and I was very kind to him. But after he had dug holes in the ground to get the gold, and killed all the elephants to get their ivory tusks, he went away secretly in his ship—without so much as saying 'Thank you.' Never again shall a white man travel through the lands of Jolliginki."

Then the King turned to some of his men who were standing near and said, "Take away this Medicine-Man—with all his animals, and lock them up in my strongest prison."

So six of the men led the Doctor and all his pets away and shut them up in a stone dungeon. The dungeon had only one little window, high up in the wall, with bars in it; and the door was strong and thick.

Then they all grew very sad; and Gub-Gub, the pig, began to cry. But Chee-Chee said he would spank him if he didn't stop that horrible noise; and he kept quiet.

"Are we all here?" asked the Doctor, after he had got used to the dim light.

"Yes, I think so," said the duck and started to count them.

"Where's Polynesia?" asked the crocodile. "She isn't here."

"Are you sure?" said the Doctor. "Look again.

Polynesia! Polynesia! Where are you?"

"I suppose she escaped," grumbled the crocodile. "Well, that's just like her!—Sneaked off into the jungle as soon as her friends got into trouble."

"I'm not that kind of a bird," said the parrot, climbing out of the pocket in the tail of the Doctor's coat. "You see, I'm small enough to get through the bars of that window; and I was afraid they would put me in a cage instead. So while the King was busy talking, I hid in the Doctor's pocket—and here I am! That's what you call a 'ruse,' " she said, smoothing down her feathers with her beak.

"Good Gracious!" cried the Doctor. "You're lucky I didn't sit on you."

"Now listen," said Polynesia, "to-night, as soon as it gets dark, I am going to creep through the bars of that window and fly over to the palace. And then—you'll see—I'll soon find a way to make the King let us all out of prison."

"Oh, what can *you* do?" said Gub-Gub, turning up his nose and beginning to cry again. "You're only a bird!"

"Quite true," said the parrot. "But do not forget that although I am only a bird, *I can talk like a man*—and I know these people."

So that night, when the moon was shining through the palm-trees and all the King's men were asleep, the parrot slipped out through the bars of the prison and flew across to the palace. The pantry window had been broken by a tennis ball the week before; and Polynesia popped in through the hole in the glass.

She heard Prince Bumpo snoring in his bedroom at the back of the palace. Then she tiptoed up the stairs till she came to the King's bedroom. She opened the door gently and peeped in.

The Queen was away at a dance that night at her cousin's; but the King was in bed fast asleep.

Polynesia crept in, very softly, and got under the bed.

Then she coughed—just the way Doctor Dolittle used to cough. Polynesia could mimic any one.

The King opened his eyes and said sleepily: "Is that you, Ermintrude?" (He thought it was the Queen come back from the dance.)

Then the parrot coughed again—loud, like a man. And the King sat up, wide awake, and said, "Who's that?"

"I am Doctor Dolittle," said the parrot—just

" 'Who's that?' "

the way the Doctor would have said it.

"What are you doing in my bedroom?" cried the King. "How dare you get out of prison! Where are you?—I don't see you."

But the parrot just laughed—a long, deep, jolly laugh, like the Doctor's.

"Stop laughing and come here at once, so I can see you," said the King.

"Foolish King!" answered Polynesia. "Have you forgotten that you are talking to John Dolittle, M.D.—the most wonderful man on earth? Of course you cannot see me. I have made myself invisible. There is nothing I cannot do. Now listen: I have come here to-night to warn you. If you don't let me and my animals travel through your kingdom, I will make you and all your people sick like the monkeys. For I can make people well: and I can make people ill—just by raising my little finger. Send your soldiers at once to open the dungeon door, or you shall have mumps before the morning sun has risen on the hills of Jolliginki."

Then the King began to tremble and was very much afraid.

"Doctor," he cried, "it shall be as you say. Do not raise your little finger, please!" And he jumped out of bed and ran to tell the soldiers to open the prison door.

As soon as he was gone, Polynesia crept downstairs and left the palace by the pantry window.

But the Queen, who was just letting herself in at the backdoor with a latchkey, saw the parrot getting out through the broken glass. And when the King came back to bed she told him what she had seen.

Then the King understood that he had been tricked, and he was dreadfully angry. He hurried back to the prison at once.

But he was too late. The door stood open. The dungeon was empty. The Doctor and all his animals were gone.

THE SEVENTH CHAPTER

THE BRIDGE OF APES

QUEEN ERMINTRUDE had never in her life seen her husband so terrible as he got that night. He gnashed his teeth with rage. He called everybody a fool. He threw his tooth-brush at the palace cat. He rushed round in his night-shirt and woke up all his army and sent them into the jungle to catch the Doctor. Then he made all his servants go too—his cooks and his gardeners and his barber and Prince Bumpo's tutor—even the Queen, who was tired from dancing in a pair of tight shoes, was packed off to help the soldiers in their search.

All this time the Doctor and his animals were running through the forest towards the Land of the Monkeys as fast as they could go.

Gub-Gub, with his short legs, soon got tired;

and the Doctor had to carry him—which made it pretty hard when they had the trunk and the hand-bag with them as well.

The King of the Jolliginki thought it would be easy for his army to find them, because the Doctor was in a strange land and would not know his way. But he was wrong; because the monkey, Chee-Chee, knew all the paths through the jungle—better even than the King's men did. And he led the Doctor and his pets to the very thickest part of the forest—a place where no man had ever been before—and hid them all in a big hollow tree between high rocks.

"We had better wait here," said Chee-Chee, "till the soldiers have gone back to bed. Then we can go on into the Land of the Monkeys."

So there they stayed the whole night through.

They often heard the King's men searching and talking in the jungle round about. But they were quite safe, for no one knew of that hiding-place but Chee-Chee—not even the other monkeys.

At last, when daylight began to come through the thick leaves overhead, they heard Queen Ermintrude saying in a very tired voice that it was no use looking any more—that they might as well go back and get some sleep.

As soon as the soldiers had all gone home, Chee-Chee brought the Doctor and his animals out of the hiding-place and they set off for the Land of the Monkeys.

It was a long, long way; and they often got very tired—especially Gub-Gub. But when he cried they gave him milk out of the cocoanuts, which he was very fond of.

They always had plenty to eat and drink; because Chee-Chee and Polynesia knew all the different kinds of fruits and vegetables that grow in the jungle, and where to find them—like dates and figs and ground-nuts and ginger and yams. They used to make their lemonade out of the juice of wild oranges, sweetened with honey which they got from the bees' nests in hollow trees. No matter what it was they asked for, Chee-Chee and Polynesia always seemed to be able to get it for them—or something like it. They even got the Doctor some tobacco one day, when he had finished what he had brought with him and wanted to smoke.

At night they slept in tents made of palm-leaves, on thick, soft beds of dried grass. And after a while they got used to walking such a lot and did not get so tired and enjoyed the life of travel very much.

But they were always glad when the night came and they stopped for their resting-time. Then the Doctor used to make a little fire of sticks; and after they had had their supper, they would sit round it in a ring, listening to Polynesia singing songs about the sea, or to Chee-Chee telling stories of the jungle.

And many of the tales that Chee-Chee told were very interesting. Because although the monkeys had no history-books of their own before Doctor Dolittle came to write them for them, they remember everything that happens by telling stories to their children. And Chee-Chee spoke of many things his grandmother had told him—tales of long, long, long ago, before Noah and the Flood,—of the days when men dressed in bear-skins and lived in holes in the rock and ate their mutton raw, because they did not know what cooking was—having never seen a fire. And he told them of the Great Mammoths and Lizards, as long as a train, that wandered over the mountains in those times, nibbling from the tree-tops. And often they got so interested listening, that when he had finished they found their fire had gone right out; and they had to scurry round to get more sticks and build a new one.

Now when the King's army had gone back and told the King that they couldn't find the Doctor, the King sent them out again and told them they must stay in the jungle till they caught him. So all this time, while the Doctor and his animals were going along towards the Land of the Monkeys, thinking themselves quite safe, they were still being followed by the King's men. If Chee-Chee had known this, he would most likely have hidden them again. But he didn't know it.

One day Chee-Chee climbed up a high rock and looked out over the tree-tops. And when he came down he said they were now quite close to the Land of the Monkeys and would soon be there.

And that same evening, sure enough, they saw Chee-Chee's cousin and a lot of other monkeys, who had not yet got sick, sitting in the trees by the edge of a swamp, looking and waiting for them. And when they saw the famous doctor really come, these monkeys made a tremendous noise, cheering and waving leaves and swinging out of the branches to greet him.

They wanted to carry his bag and his trunk and everything he had—and one of the bigger ones even carried Gub-Gub who had got tired again. Then two of them rushed on in front to tell the sick monkeys that the great doctor had come at last.

But the King's men, who were still following, had heard the noise of the monkeys cheering; and they at last knew where the Doctor was, and hastened on to catch him.

The big monkey carrying Gub-Gub was coming along behind slowly, and he saw the Captain of the army sneaking through the trees. So he hurried after the Doctor and told him to run.

Then they all ran harder than they had ever run in their lives; and the King's men, coming after them, began to run too; and the Captain ran hardest of all.

Then the Doctor tripped over his medicine-bag and fell down in the mud, and the Captain thought he would surely catch him this time.

But the Captain had very long ears—though his hair was very short. And as he sprang forward to take hold of the Doctor, one of his ears

"Cheering and waving leaves and swinging out of the branches to greet him"

caught fast in a tree; and the rest of the army had to stop and help him.

By this time the Doctor had picked himself up, and on they went again, running and running. And Chee-Chee shouted, "It's all right! We haven't far to go now!"

But before they could get into the Land of the Monkeys, they came to a steep cliff with a river flowing below. This was the end of the Kingdom of Jolliginki; and the Land of the Monkeys was on the other side—across the river.

And Jip, the dog, looked down over the edge of the steep, steep cliff and said, "Golly! How are we ever going to get across?"

"Oh, dear!" said Gub-Gub. "The King's men are quite close now—Look at them! I am afraid we are going to be taken back to prison again." And he began to weep.

But the big monkey who was carrying the pig dropped him on the ground and cried out to the other monkeys, "Boys—a bridge! Quick!—Make a bridge! We've only a minute to do it. They've got the Captain loose, and he's coming on like a deer. Get lively! A bridge! A bridge!"

The Doctor began to wonder what they were going to make a bridge out of, and he gazed around to see if they had any boards hidden any place.

But when he looked back at the cliff, there, hanging across the river, was a bridge all ready for him—made of living monkeys! For while his back was turned, the monkeys—quick as a flash—had made themselves into a bridge, just by holding hands and feet.

And the big one shouted to the Doctor, "Walk over! Walk over—all of you—hurry!"

Gub-Gub was a bit scared, walking on such a narrow bridge at that dizzy height above the river. But he got over all right; and so did all of them.

John Dolittle was the last to cross. And just as he was getting to the other side, the King's men came rushing up to the edge of the cliff.

Then they shook their fists and yelled with rage. For they saw they were too late. The Doctor and all his animals were safe in the Land of the Monkeys and the bridge was pulled across to the other side.

Then Chee-Chee turned to the Doctor and said, "Many great explorers and gray-bearded naturalists have lain long weeks hidden in the jungle waiting to see the monkeys do that trick.

But we never let a white man get a glimpse of it before. You are the first to see the famous 'Bridge of Apes.'"

And the Doctor felt very pleased.

"John Dolittle was the last to cross"

THE EIGHTH CHAPTER

THE LEADER OF THE LIONS

JOHN DOLITTLE now became dreadfully, awfully busy. He found hundreds and thousands of monkeys sick—gorillas, orangutans, chimpanzees, dog-faced baboons, marmosets, gray monkeys, red ones—all kinds. And many had died.

The first thing he did was to separate the sick ones from the well ones. Then he got Chee-Chee and his cousin to build him a little house of grass. The next thing: he made all the monkeys who were still well come and be vaccinated.

And for three days and three nights the monkeys kept coming from the jungles and the valleys and the hills to the little house of grass, where the Doctor sat all day and all night, vaccinating and vaccinating.

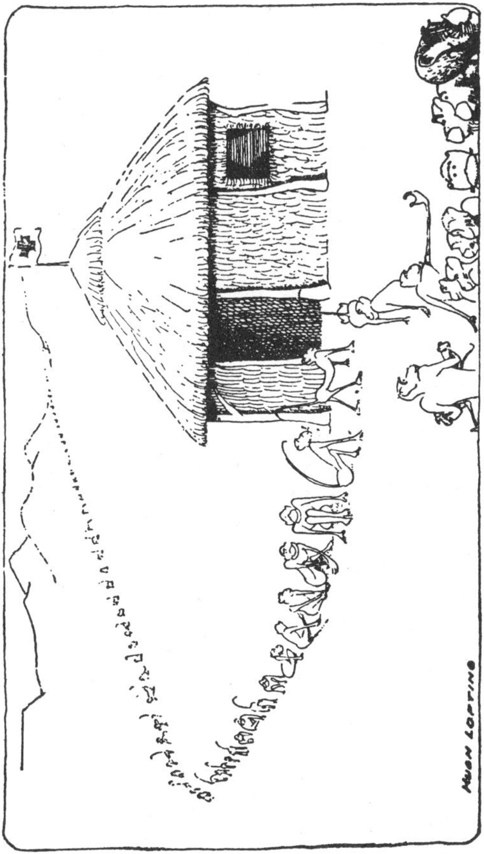

"He made all the monkeys who were still well come and be vaccinated"

Then he had another house made—a big one, with a lot of beds in it; and he put all the sick ones in this house.

But so many were sick, there were not enough well ones to do the nursing. So he sent messages to the other animals, like the lions and the leopards and the antelopes, to come and help with the nursing.

But the Leader of the Lions was a very proud creature. And when he came to the Doctor's big house full of beds he seemed angry and scornful.

"Do you dare to ask me, Sir?" he said, glaring at the Doctor. "Do you dare to ask me—*ME, the King of Beasts*, to wait on a lot of dirty monkeys? Why, I wouldn't even eat them between meals!"

Although the lion looked very terrible, the Doctor tried hard not to seem afraid of him.

"I didn't ask you to eat them," he said quietly. "And besides, they're not dirty. They've all had a bath this morning. *Your* coat looks as though it needed brushing—badly. Now listen, and I'll tell you something: the day may come when the lions get sick. And if you don't help the other animals now, the lions may find themselves left all alone when *they* are in trouble. That often happens to proud people."

"The Doctor tried hard not to seem afraid of him"

"The lions are never *in* trouble—they only *make* trouble," said the Leader, turning up his nose. And he stalked away into the jungle, feeling he had been rather smart and clever.

Then the leopards got proud too and said they wouldn't help. And then of course the antelopes—although they were too shy and timid to be rude to the Doctor like the lion—*they* pawed the ground, and smiled foolishly, and said they had never been nurses before.

And now the poor Doctor was worried frantic, wondering where he could get help enough to take care of all these thousands of monkeys in bed.

But the Leader of the Lions, when he got back to his den, saw his wife, the Queen Lioness, come running out to meet him with her hair untidy.

"One of the cubs won't eat," she said. "I don't know *what* to do with him. He hasn't taken a thing since last night."

And she began to cry and shake with nervousness—for she was a good mother, even though she was a lioness.

So the Leader went into his den and looked at his children—two very cunning little cubs, lying on the floor. And one of them seemed quite poorly.

Then the lion told his wife, quite proudly, just what he had said to the Doctor. And she got so angry she nearly drove him out of the den.

"You never *did* have a grain of sense!" she screamed. "All the animals from here to the Indian Ocean are talking about this wonderful man, and how he can cure any kind of sickness, and how kind he is—the only man in the whole world who can talk the language of the animals! And now, *now*—when we have a sick baby on our hands, you must go and offend him! You great booby! Nobody but a fool is ever rude to a *good* doctor. You—," and she started pulling her husband's hair.

"Go back to him at once," she yelled, "and tell him you're sorry. And take all the other empty-headed lions with you—and those stupid leopards and antelopes. Then do everything the Doctor tells you. Work as hard as you can! And perhaps he will be kind enough to come and see the cub later. Now be off!—*Hurry*, I tell you! You're not fit to be a father!"

And she went into the den next door, where another mother-lion lived, and told her all about it.

So the Leader of the Lions went back to the Doctor and said, "I happened to be passing this way and thought I'd look in. Got any help yet?"

"No," said the Doctor. "I haven't. And I'm dreadfully worried."

"Help's pretty hard to get these days," said the lion. "Animals don't seem to want to work any more. You can't blame them—in a way. . . . Well, seeing you're in difficulties, I don't mind doing what I can—just to oblige you—so long as I don't have to wash the creatures. And I have told all the other hunting animals to come and do their share. The leopards should be here any minute now. . . . Oh, and by the way, we've got a sick cub at home. I don't think there's much the matter with him myself. But the wife is anxious. If you are around that way this evening, you might take a look at him, will you?"

Then the Doctor was very happy; for all the lions and the leopards and the antelopes and the giraffes and the zebras—all the animals of the forests and the mountains and the plains—came to help him in his work. There were so many of them that he had to send some away, and only kept the cleverest.

And now very soon the monkeys began to get better. At the end of a week the big house full of beds were half empty. And at the end of the second week the last monkey had got well.

Then the Doctor's work was done; and he was so tired he went to bed and slept for three days without even turning over.

THE NINTH CHAPTER
THE MONKEYS' COUNCIL

CHEE-CHEE stood outside the Doctor's door, keeping everybody away till he woke up. Then John Dolittle told the monkeys that he must now go back to Puddleby.

They were very surprised at this; for they had thought that he was going to stay with them forever. And that night all the monkeys got together in the jungle to talk it over.

And the Chief Chimpanzee rose up and said, "Why is it the good man is going away? Is he not happy here with us?"

But none of them could answer him.

Then the Grand Gorilla got up and said, "I think we all should go to him and ask him to stay. Perhaps if we make him a new house and a bigger bed, and promise him plenty of monkey-servants to work for him and to make life pleasant for him—perhaps then he will not wish to go."

Then Chee-Chee got up; and all the others whispered, "Sh! Look! Chee-Chee, the great Traveler, is about to speak!"

"Then the Grand Gorilla got up"

And Chee-Chee said to the other monkeys, "My friends, I am afraid it is useless to ask the Doctor to stay. He owes money in Puddleby; and he says he must go back and pay it."

And the monkeys asked him, "What is *money*?"

Then Chee-Chee told them that in Doctor Dolittle's country you could get nothing without money;

you could *do* nothing without money—that it was almost impossible to *live* without money.

And some of them asked, "But can you not even eat and drink without paying?"

But Chee-Chee shook his head. And then he told them that even he, when he was with the organ-grinder, had been made to ask the children for money.

And the Chief Chimpanzee turned to the Oldest Orangutan and said, "Cousin, surely these Men be strange creatures! Who would wish to live in such a land? My gracious, how paltry!"

Then Chee-Chee said, "When we were coming to you we had no boat to cross the sea in and no money to buy food to eat on our journey. So a man lent us some biscuits; and we said we would pay him when we came back. And we borrowed a boat from a sailor; but it was broken on the rocks when we reached the shores of Africa. Now the Doctor says he must go back and get the sailor another boat—because the man was poor and his ship was all he had."

And the monkeys were all silent for a while, sitting quite still upon the ground and thinking hard.

At last the Biggest Baboon got up and said,

"I do not think we ought to let this good man leave our land till we have given him a fine present to take with him, so that he may know we are grateful for all that he has done for us."

And a little, tiny red monkey who was sitting up in a tree shouted down, "I think that too!"

And then they all cried out, making a great noise, "Yes, yes. Let us give him the finest present a visitor to our country ever had!"

Now they began to wonder and ask one another what would be the best thing to give him. And one said, "Fifty bags of cocoanuts!" And another—"A hundred bunches of bananas!—At least he shall not have to buy his fruit in the Land Where You Pay to Eat!"

But Chee-Chee told them that all these things would be too heavy to carry so far and would go bad before half was eaten.

"If you want to please him," he said, "give him an animal. You may be sure he will be kind to it. Give him some rare animal they have not got in the menageries."

And the monkeys asked him, "What are *menageries?*"

Then Chee-Chee explained to them that menageries were places where animals were put in cages for people to come and look at. And the monkeys were very shocked and said to one another, "These Men are like thoughtless young ones—stupid and easily amused. Sh! It is a prison he means."

So then they asked Chee-Chee what rare animal it could be that they should give the Doctor—one the people in his country had not seen before. And the Major of the Marmosets asked, "Have they an iguana over there?"

But Chee-Chee said, "Yes, there is one in the London Zoo."

And another asked, "Have they an okapi?"

But Chee-Chee said, "Yes. In Belgium, where my organ-grinder took me five years ago, they had an okapi in a big city they call Antwerp."

And another asked, "Have they a pushmi-pullyu?"

Then Chee-Chee said, "No. No man from the Doctor's country has ever seen a pushmi-pullyu. Let us give him that."

THE TENTH CHAPTER

THE RAREST ANIMAL OF ALL

PUSHMI-PULLYUS are now extinct. That means, there aren't any more. But long ago, when Doctor Dolittle was alive, there were some of them still left in the deepest jungles of Africa; and even then they were very, very scarce. They had no tail, but a head at each end, and sharp horns on each head. They were very shy and terribly hard to catch. The black men get most of their animals by sneaking up behind them while they are not looking. But you could not do this with the pushmi-pullyu—because, no matter which way you came towards him, he was always facing you. And besides, only one half of him slept at a time. The other head was always awake—and watching. This was why they were never caught and never seen in Zoos. Though many of the greatest huntsmen and the cleverest menagerie-keepers spent years of their lives searching through the jungles in all weathers for pushmi-pullyus, not a single one had ever been caught. Even then, years ago, he was the only animal in the world with two heads.

Well, the monkeys set out hunting for this animal through the forest. And after they had gone a good many miles, one of them found peculiar footprints near the edge of a river; and they knew that a pushmi-pullyu must be very near that spot.

Then they went along the bank of the river a little way and they saw a place where the grass was high and thick; and they guessed that he was in there.

So they all joined hands and made a great circle round the high grass. The pushmi-pullyu heard them coming; and he tried hard to break through the ring of monkeys. But he couldn't do it. When he saw that it was no use trying to escape, he sat down and waited to see what they wanted.

They asked him if he would go with Doctor Dolittle and be put on show in the Land Across the Ocean.

But he shook both his heads hard and said, "Certainly not!"

They explained to him that he would not be shut up in a menagerie but would just be looked at. They told him that the Doctor was a very kind man but hadn't any money; and people would pay to see a two-headed animal and the Doctor would get rich and could pay for the boat he had borrowed to come to Africa in.

But he answered, "No. You know how shy I am—I hate being stared at." And he almost began to cry.

Then for three days they tried to persuade him.

And at the end of the third day he said he would come with them and see what kind of a man the Doctor was, first.

So the monkeys traveled back with the pushmi-pullyu. And when they came to where the Doctor's little house of grass was, they knocked on the door.

The duck, who was packing the trunk, said, "Come in!"

And Chee-Chee very proudly took the animal inside and showed him to the Doctor.

"What in the world is it?" asked John Dolittle,

gazing at the strange creature.

"Lord save us!" cried the duck. "How does it make up its mind?"

"It doesn't look to me as though it had any," said Jip, the dog.

"This, Doctor," said Chee-Chee, "is the pushmi-pullyu—the rarest animal of the African jungles, the only two-headed beast in the world! Take him home with you and your fortune's made. People will pay any money to see him."

"But I don't want any money," said the Doctor.

"Yes, you do," said Dab-Dab, the duck. "Don't you remember how we had to pinch and scrape to pay the butcher's bill in Puddleby? And how are you going to get the sailor the new boat you spoke of—unless we have the money to buy it?"

"I was going to make him one," said the Doctor.

"Oh, do be sensible!" cried Dab-Dab. "Where would you get all the wood and the nails to make one with?—And besides, what are we going to live on? We shall be poorer than ever when we get back. Chee-Chee's perfectly right: take the funny-looking thing along, do!"

"Well, perhaps there is something in what you

" 'Lord save us!' cried the duck.
'How does it make up its mind?' "

say," murmured the Doctor. "It certainly would make a nice new kind of pet. But does the er—what-do-you-call-it really want to go abroad?"

"Yes, I'll go," said the pushmi-pullyu who saw at once, from the Doctor's face, that he was a man to be trusted. "You have been so kind to the animals here—and the monkeys tell me that I am the only one who will do. But you must promise me that if I do not like it in the Land Across the Ocean you will send me back."

"Why, certainly—of course, of course," said the Doctor. "Excuse me, surely you are related to the Deer Family, are you not?"

"Yes," said the pushmi-pullyu—"to the Abyssinian Gazelles and the Asiatic Chamois—on my mother's side. My father's great-grandfather was the last of the Unicorns."

"Most interesting!" murmured the Doctor; and he took a book out of the trunk which Dab-Dab was packing and began turning the pages. "Let us see if Buffon says anything—"

"I notice," said the duck, "that you only talk with one of your mouths. Can't the other head talk as well?"

"Oh, yes," said the pushmi-pullyu. "But I keep the other mouth for eating—mostly. In that way

I can talk while I am eating without being rude. Our people have always been very polite."

When the packing was finished and everything was ready to start, the monkeys gave a grand party for the Doctor, and all the animals of the jungle came. And they had pineapples and mangoes and honey and all sorts of good things to eat and drink.

After they had all finished eating, the Doctor got up and said, "My friends: I am not clever at speaking long words after dinner, like some men; and I have just eaten many fruits and much honey. But I wish to tell you that I am very sad at leaving your beautiful country. Because I have things to do in my own beautiful country, I must go. After I have gone, remember never to let the flies settle on your food before you eat it; and do not sleep on the ground when the rains are coming. I—er—er—I hope you will all live happily ever after."

When the Doctor stopped speaking and sat down, all the monkeys clapped their hands a long time and said to one another, "Let it be remembered always among our people that he sat and ate with us, here, under the trees. For surely he is the Greatest of Men!"

And the Grand Gorilla, who had the strength of seven horses in his hairy arms, rolled a great rock up to the head of the table and said, "This stone for all time shall mark the spot."

And even to this day, in the heart of the jungle, that stone still is there. And monkey-mothers, passing through the forest with their families, still point down at it from the branches and whisper to their children, "Sh! There it is—look—where the Good Man from The Land Across the Ocean sat and ate food with us in the Year of the Great Sickness!"

Then, when the party was over, the Doctor and his pets started out to go back to the seashore. And all the monkeys went with him as far as the edge of their country, carrying his trunk and bags, to see him off.

THE ELEVENTH CHAPTER
THE BLACK PRINCE

BY the edge of the river they stopped and said farewell.

This took a long time, because all those thousands of monkeys wanted to shake John Dolittle by the hand.

Afterwards, when the Doctor and his pets were going on alone, Polynesia said, "We must tread softly and talk low as we go through the land of the Jolliginki. If the King should hear us, he will send his soldiers to catch us again; for I am sure he is still very angry over the trick I played on him."

"What I am wondering," said the Doctor, "is where we are going to get another boat to go home in. . . . Oh well, perhaps we'll find one lying about on the beach that nobody is using.

'Never lift your foot till you come to the stile.' "

One day, while they were passing through a very thick part of the forest, Chee-Chee went ahead of them to look for cocoanuts. And while he was away, the Doctor and the rest of the animals, who did not know the jungle-paths so well, got lost in the deep woods. They wandered around and around but could not find their way down to the seashore.

Chee-Chee, when he could not see them anywhere, was terribly upset. He climbed high trees and looked out from the top branches to try and see the Doctor's high hat; he waved and shouted; he called to all the animals by name. But it was no use. They seemed to have disappeared altogether.

Indeed they had lost their way very badly. They had strayed a long way off the path, and the jungle was so thick with bushes and creepers and vines that sometimes they could hardly move at all, and the Doctor had to take out his pocket-knife and cut his way along. They stumbled into wet, boggy places; they got all tangled up in thick convolvulus-runners; they scratched themselves on thorns, and twice they nearly lost the medicine-bag in the under-brush. There seemed no end to their troubles; and nowhere could they come upon a path.

At last, after blundering about like this for many days, getting their clothes torn and their faces covered with mud, they walked right into the King's back-garden by mistake. The King's men came running up at once and caught them.

But Polynesia flew into a tree in the garden, without anybody seeing her, and hid herself. The Doctor and the rest were taken before the King.

"Ha, ha!" cried the King. "So you are caught again! This time you shall not escape. Take them all back to prison and put double locks on the door. This Medicine-Man shall scrub my kitchen-floor for the rest of his life!"

So the Doctor and his pets were led back to prison and locked up. And the Doctor was told that in the morning he must begin scrubbing the kitchen-floor.

They were all very unhappy.

"This is a great nuisance," said the Doctor. "I really must get back to Puddleby. That poor sailor will think I've stolen his ship if I don't get home soon. . . . I wonder if those hinges are loose."

But the door was very strong and firmly locked. There seemed no chance of getting out. Then Gub-Gub began to cry again.

All this time Polynesia was still sitting in the tree in the palace-garden. She was saying nothing and blinking her eyes.

This was always a very bad sign with Polynesia. Whenever she said nothing and blinked her eyes, it meant that somebody had been making trouble, and she was thinking out some way to put things right. People who made trouble for Polynesia or her friends were nearly always sorry for it afterwards.

Presently she spied Chee-Chee swinging through the trees still looking for the Doctor. When Chee-Chee saw her, he came into her tree and asked her what had become of him.

"The Doctor and all the animals have been caught by the King's men and locked up again," whispered Polynesia. "We lost our way in the jungle and blundered into the palace-garden by mistake."

"But couldn't you guide them?" asked Chee-Chee; and he began to scold the parrot for letting them get lost while he was away looking for the cocoanuts.

"It was all that stupid pig's fault," said Polynesia. "He would keep running off the path hunting for ginger-roots. And I was kept so busy catching him and bringing him back, that I turned to the left, instead of the right, when we reached the swamp.—Sh!—Look! There's Prince Bumpo coming into the garden! He must not see us.—Don't move, whatever you do!"

And there, sure enough, was Prince Bumpo, the King's son, opening the garden-gate. He carried a book of fairy-tales under his arm. He came strolling down the gravel-walk, humming a sad song, till he reached a stone seat right under the tree where the parrot and the monkey were hiding. Then he lay down on the seat and began reading the fairy-stories to himself.

Chee-Chee and Polynesia watched him, keeping very quiet and still.

After a while the King's son laid the book down and sighed a weary sigh. "If only I didn't have these spots on my face!" said he, with a dreamy, far-away look in his eyes.

Then the parrot, talking in a small, high voice like a little girl, said aloud, "Bumpo, some one might turn thee into a prince without spots perchance."

The King's son started up off the seat and looked all around.

"What is this I hear?" he cried. "Methought the sweet music of a fairy's silver voice rang from yonder bower! Strange!"

"Worthy Prince," said Polynesia, keeping very still so Bumpo couldn't see her, "thou sayest winged words of truth. For 'tis I, Tripsitinka, the Queen of the Fairies, that speak to thee. I am hiding in a rose-bud."

"Oh tell me, Fairy-Queen," cried Bumpo, clasping his hands in joy, "who is it can remove my spots?"

"In thy father's prison," said the parrot, "there lies a famous wizard, John Dolittle by name. Many things he knows of medicine and magic, and mighty deeds has he performed. Yet thy kingly father leaves him languishing long and lingering hours. Go to him, brave Bumpo, secretly, when the sun has set; and behold, thou shalt be made the finest prince without spots that ever won fair lady! I have said enough. I must now go back to Fairyland. Farewell!"

"Farewell!" cried the Prince. "A thousand thanks, good Tripsitinka!"

And he sat down on the seat again with a

smile upon his face, waiting for the sun to set.

THE TWELFTH CHAPTER
MEDICINE AND MAGIC

VERY, very quietly, making sure that no one should see her, Polynesia then slipped out at the back of the tree and flew across to the prison.

She found Gub-Gub poking his nose through the bars of the window, trying to sniff the cooking-smells that came from the palace-kitchen. She told the pig to bring the Doctor to the window because she wanted to speak to him. So Gub-Gub went and woke the Doctor who was taking a nap.

"Listen," whispered the parrot, when John Dolittle's face appeared: "Prince Bumpo is coming here to-night to see you. And you've got to find some way to help him get rid of the pimples on his face. But be sure to make him promise you first that he will open the prison-door and find a ship for you to cross the sea in."

"This is all very well," said the Doctor. "But it isn't so easy to get rid of a teenager's pimples in the blink of an eye. You speak as though he were a dress to be re-dyed. It's not so simple. 'Shall the leopard change his spots, or the Ethiopian his skin,' you know?"

"He's not a leopard!" said Polynesia impatiently. "You *must* help the poor young man. Think of a way—think hard. You've got plenty of medicines left in the bag. He'll do anything for you if you remove his pimples. It is your only chance to get out of prison."

"Well, I suppose it *might* be possible," said the Doctor. "Let me see—," and he went over to his medicine-bag, murmuring something about "liberated chlorine on animal-pigment—perhaps zinc-ointment, as a temporary measure, spread thick—"

Well, that night Prince Bumpo came secretly to the Doctor in prison and said to him, "Doctor, I am an unhappy prince. Years ago I went in search of The Sleeping Beauty, whom I had read of in a book. And having traveled through the world many days, riding on a horse and wearing shining armor and gauntlets of steel, like all princes do, I at last found her and kissed the lady very gently to awaken her—as the book said I should. 'Tis true indeed that she awoke. But when she saw my face she cried out, 'Oh, no, you have spots!' And she ran away and wouldn't marry me—but went to sleep again somewhere else. Just because of my *spots*! So I came back, full of sadness, to my father's kingdom. Now I hear that you are a wonderful magician and have many powerful potions. So I come to you for help. If you will remove my spots immediately, so that I may go back to The Sleeping Beauty, I will give you half my kingdom and anything besides you ask."

"Prince Bumpo," said the Doctor, looking thoughtfully at the bottles in his medicine-bag, "supposing I changed the color of your hair—would not that do instead to make you happy?"

"No, my hair is fine," said Bumpo. "I must be free of *spots*!"

"You know it is very hard to remove pimples in a hurry," said the Doctor—"one of the hardest things a magician can do. You only have them on your face, do you?"

"Yes," said Bumpo.

"And you want to have *every* pimple removed?" asked the Doctor.

"Yes, every one," said Bumpo.

"Well, I will do what I can for you," said the Doctor. "You will have to be very patient though—you know with some medicines you can never be very sure. I might have to try two or three times. You have a strong skin—yes? Well that's all right. Now come over here by the light—Oh, but before I do anything, you must first go down to the beach and get a ship ready, with food in it, to take me across the sea. Do not speak a word of this to any one. And when I have done as you ask, you must let me and all my animals out of prison. Promise—by the crown of Jolliginki!"

So the Prince promised and went away to get a ship ready at the seashore.

When he came back and said that it was done, the Doctor asked Dab-Dab to bring a basin. Then he mixed a lot of medicines in the basin and told Bumpo to dip his face in it.

The Prince leaned down and put his face in—right up to the ears.

He held it there a long time—so long that the Doctor seemed to get dreadfully anxious and fidgety, standing first on one leg and then on the other, looking at all the bottles he had used for the mixture, and reading the labels on them again and again. A strong smell filled the prison, like the smell of brown paper burning.

At last the Prince lifted his face up out of the basin, breathing very hard. And all the animals cried out in surprise.

For there was not one pimple left on the Prince's face!

When John Dolittle lent him a little looking-glass to see himself in, he sang for joy and began dancing around the prison. But the Doctor asked him not to make so much noise about it; and when he had closed his medicine-bag in a hurry he told him to open the prison-door.

Bumpo begged that he might keep the looking-glass, as it was the only one in the Kingdom of Jolliginki, and he wanted to look at himself all day long. But the Doctor said he needed it to shave with.

Then the Prince, taking a bunch of copper keys from his pocket, undid the great double locks. And the Doctor with all his animals ran as fast as they could down to the seashore; while Bumpo leaned against the wall of the empty dungeon, smiling after them happily, his big spot-free face shining like polished ebony in the light of the moon.

When they came to the beach they saw Polynesia and Chee-Chee waiting for them on the rocks near the ship.

"I feel sorry about Bumpo," said the Doctor. "I am afraid that medicine I used will never last. Most likely he will find some pimples have returned when he wakes up in the morning—that's one reason why I didn't like to leave the mirror with him. But then again, he *might* stay pimple-free—I had never used that mixture before. To tell the truth, I was surprised, myself, that it worked so well. But I had to do something, didn't I?—I couldn't possibly scrub the King's kitchen for the rest of my life. It was such a dirty kitchen!—I could see it from the prison-window.—Well, well!—Poor Bumpo!"

"Oh, of course he will know we were just joking with him," said the parrot.

"They had no business to lock us up," said Dab-Dab, waggling her tail angrily. "We never did them any harm. Serve him right, if his spots come back! I hope he gets lots of them."

"But *he* didn't have anything to do with it," said the Doctor. "It was the King, his father, who had us locked up—it wasn't Bumpo's fault . . . I wonder if I ought to go back and apologize—Oh, well—I'll send him some candy when I get to Puddleby. And who knows?—he may stay free of pimples after all."

"The Sleeping Beauty would never have him, even if he did," said Dab-Dab. "He looked better the way he was, with a few spots, I thought. But he'd never be anything but ugly, with or without spots."

"Still, he had a good heart," said the Doctor—"romantic, of course—but a good heart. After all, 'handsome is as handsome does.'"

"I don't believe the poor booby found The Sleeping Beauty at all," said Jip, the dog. "Most likely he kissed some farmer's fat wife who was taking a snooze under an apple-tree. Can't blame her for running away! I wonder who he'll go and kiss this time. Silly business!"

Then the pushmi-pullyu, the white mouse, Gub-Gub, Dab-Dab, Jip and the owl, Too-Too, went on to the ship with the Doctor. But Chee-Chee, Polynesia and the crocodile stayed behind, because Africa was their proper home, the land where they were born.

And when the Doctor stood upon the boat,

he looked over the side across the water. And then he remembered that they had no one with them to guide them back to Puddleby.

The wide, wide sea looked terribly big and lonesome in the moonlight; and he began to wonder if they would lose their way when they passed out of sight of land.

But even while he was wondering, they heard a strange whispering noise, high in the air, coming through the night. And the animals all stopped saying Good-by and listened.

The noise grew louder and bigger. It seemed to be coming nearer to them—a sound like the autumn wind blowing through the leaves of a poplar-tree, or a great, great rain beating down upon a roof.

And Jip, with his nose pointing and his tail quite straight, said, "Birds!—millions of them—flying fast—that's it!"

And then they all looked up. And there, streaming across the face of the moon, like a huge swarm of tiny ants, they could see thousands and thousands of little birds. Soon the whole sky seemed full of them, and still more kept coming—more and more. There were so many that for a little they covered the whole moon so it could not shine, and the sea grew dark and black—like when a storm-cloud passes over the sun.

And presently all these birds came down close, skimming over the water and the land; and the night-sky was left clear above, and the moon shone as before. Still never a call nor a cry nor a song they made—no sound but this great rustling of feathers which grew greater now than ever. When they began to settle on the sands, along the ropes of the ship—anywhere and everywhere except the trees—the Doctor could see that they had blue wings and white breasts and very short, feathered legs. As soon as they had all found a place to sit, suddenly, there was no noise left anywhere—all was quiet; all was still.

And in the silent moonlight John Dolittle spoke: "I had no idea that we had been in Africa so long. It will be nearly summer when we get home. For these are the swallows going back. Swallows, I thank you for waiting for us. It is very thoughtful of you. Now we need not be afraid that we will lose our way upon the sea. . . . Pull up the anchor and set the sail!"

When the ship moved out upon the water, those who stayed behind, Chee-Chee, Polynesia

"Crying bitterly and waving till the ship was out of sight"

and the crocodile, grew terribly sad. For never in their lives had they known any one they liked so well as Doctor John Dolittle of Puddleby-on-the-Marsh.

And after they had called Good-by to him again and again and again, they still stood there upon the rocks, crying bitterly and waving till the ship was out of sight.

THE THIRTEENTH CHAPTER

RED SAILS AND BLUE WINGS

SAILING homeward, the Doctor's ship had to pass the coast of Barbary. This coast is the sea-shore of the Great Desert. It is a wild, lonely place—all sand and stones. And it was here that the Barbary pirates lived.

These pirates, a bad lot of men, used to wait for sailors to be shipwrecked on their shores. And often, if they saw a boat passing, they would come out in their fast sailing-ships and chase it. When they caught a boat like this at sea, they would steal everything on it; and after they had taken the people off they would sink the ship and sail back to Barbary singing songs and feeling proud of the mischief they had done. Then they used to make the people they had caught write home to their friends for money.

And if the friends sent no money, the pirates often threw the people into the sea.

Now one sunshiny day the Doctor and Dab-Dab were walking up and down on the ship for exercise; a nice fresh wind was blowing the boat along, and everybody was happy. Presently Dab-Dab saw the sail of another ship a long way behind them on the edge of the sea. It was a red sail.

"I don't like the look of that sail," said Dab-Dab. "I have a feeling it isn't a friendly ship. I am afraid there is more trouble coming to us."

Jip, who was lying near taking a nap in the sun, began to growl and talk in his sleep.

"I smell roast beef cooking," he mumbled—"underdone roast beef—with brown gravy over it."

"Good gracious!" cried the Doctor. "What's the matter with the dog? Is he *smelling* in his sleep—as well as talking?"

"I suppose he is," said Dab-Dab. "All dogs can smell in their sleep."

"But what is he smelling?" asked the Doctor. "There is no roast beef cooking on our ship."

"No," said Dab-Dab. "The roast beef must be on that other ship over there."

“But that’s ten miles away,” said the Doctor. “He couldn’t smell that far surely!”

“Oh, yes, he could,” said Dab-Dab. “You ask him.”

Then Jip, still fast asleep, began to growl again and his lip curled up angrily, showing his clean, white teeth.

“I smell bad men,” he growled—“the worst men I ever smelt. I smell trouble. I smell a fight—six bad scoundrels fighting against one brave man. I want to help him. Woof—oo—WOOF!” Then he barked, loud, and woke himself up with a surprised look on his face.

“See!” cried Dab-Dab. “That boat is nearer now. You can count its three big sails—all red. Whoever it is, they are coming after us. . . . I wonder who they are.”

“They are bad sailors,” said Jip; “and their ship is very swift. They are surely the pirates of Barbary.”

“Well, we must put up more sails on our boat,” said the Doctor, “so we can go faster and get away from them. Run downstairs, Jip, and fetch me all the sails you see.”

The dog hurried downstairs and dragged up every sail he could find.

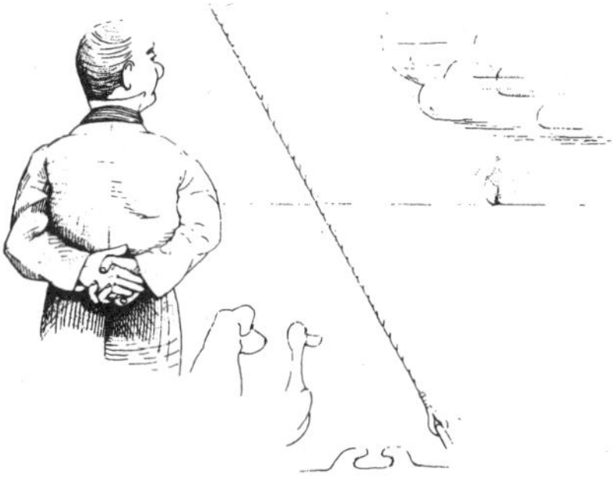

" 'They are surely the pirates of Barbary' "

But even when all these were put up on the masts to catch the wind, the boat did not go nearly as fast as the pirates'—which kept coming on behind, closer and closer.

"This is a poor ship the Prince gave us," said Gub-Gub, the pig—"the slowest he could find, I should think. Might as well try to win a race in a soup-tureen as hope to get away from them in this old barge. Look how near they are now!—You can see the mustaches on the faces of the men—six of them. What are we going to do?"

Then the Doctor asked Dab-Dab to fly up and tell the swallows that pirates were coming after them in a swift ship, and what should he do about it.

When the swallows heard this, they all came down on to the Doctor's ship; and they told him to unravel some pieces of long rope and make them into a lot of thin strings as quickly as he could. Then the ends of these strings were tied on to the front of the ship; and the swallows took hold of the strings with their feet and flew off, pulling the boat along.

And although swallows are not very strong when only one or two are by themselves, it is different when there are a great lot of them together. And there, tied to the Doctor's ship, were a thousand strings; and two thousand swallows were pulling on each string—all terribly swift fliers.

And in a moment the Doctor found himself traveling so fast he had to hold his hat on with both hands; for he felt as though the ship itself were flying through waves that frothed and boiled with speed.

And all the animals on the ship began to laugh and dance about in the rushing air, for when they looked back at the pirates' ship, they could see that it was growing smaller now, instead of bigger. The red sails were being left far, far behind.

THE FOURTEENTH CHAPTER
THE RATS' WARNING

DRAGGING a ship through the sea is hard work. And after two or three hours the swallows began to get tired in the wings and short of breath. Then they sent a message down to the Doctor to say that they would have to take a rest soon; and that they would pull the boat over to an island not far off, and hide it in a deep bay till they had got breath enough to go on.

And presently the Doctor saw the island they had spoken of. It had a very beautiful, high, green mountain in the middle of it. When the ship had sailed safely into the bay where it could not be seen from the open sea, the Doctor said he would get off on to the island to look for water—because there was none left to drink on his ship. And he told all the animals to get out too and romp on the grass to stretch their legs.

Now as they were getting off, the Doctor noticed that a whole lot of rats were coming up from downstairs and leaving the ship as well. Jip started to run after them, because chasing rats had always been his favorite game. But the Doctor told him to stop.

And one big black rat, who seemed to want to say something to the Doctor, now crept forward timidly along the rail, watching the dog out of the corner of his eye. And after he had coughed nervously two or three times, and cleaned his whiskers and wiped his mouth, he said, "Ahem—er—you know of course that all ships have rats in them, Doctor, do you not?"

And the Doctor said, "Yes."

"And you have heard that rats always leave a sinking ship?"

"Yes," said the Doctor—"so I've been told."

"People," said the rat, "always speak of it with a sneer—as though it were something disgraceful. But you can't blame us, can you? After all, who *would* stay on a sinking ship, if he could get off it?"

"It's very natural," said the Doctor—"very natural. I quite understand. . . . Was there—was

" 'And you have heard that rats always leave a sinking ship?' "

there anything else you wished to say?"

"Yes," said the rat. "I've come to tell you that we are leaving this one. But we wanted to warn you before we go. This is a bad ship you have here. It isn't safe. The sides aren't strong enough. Its boards are rotten. Before tomorrow night it will sink to the bottom of the sea."

"But how do you know?" asked the Doctor.

"We always know," answered the rat. "The tips of our tails get that tingly feeling—like when your foot's asleep. This morning, at six o'clock, while I was getting breakfast, my tail suddenly began to tingle. At first I thought it was my rheumatism coming back. So I went and asked my aunt how she felt—you remember her?—the long, piebald rat, rather skinny, who came to see you in Puddleby last Spring with jaundice? Well—and she said *her* tail was tingling like everything! Then we knew, for sure, that this boat was going to sink in less than two days; and we all made up our minds to leave it as soon as we got near enough to any land. It's a bad ship, Doctor. Don't sail in it any more, or you'll be surely drowned. . . . Good-by! We are now going to look for a good place to live on this island."

"Good-by!" said the Doctor. "And thank you very much for coming to tell me. Very considerate of you—very! Give my regards to your aunt. I remember her perfectly. . . . Leave that rat alone, Jip! Come here! Lie down!"

So then the Doctor and all his animals went off, carrying pails and saucepans, to look for water on the island, while the swallows took their rest.

"I wonder what is the name of this island," said the Doctor, as he was climbing up the mountainside. "It seems a pleasant place. What a lot of birds there are!"

"Why, these are the Canary Islands," said Dab-Dab. "Don't you hear the canaries singing?"

The Doctor stopped and listened.

"Why, to be sure—of course!" he said. "How stupid of me! I wonder if they can tell us where to find water."

And presently the canaries, who had heard all about Doctor Dolittle from birds of passage, came and led him to a beautiful spring of cool, clear water where the canaries used to take their bath; and they showed him lovely meadows where the bird-seed grew and all the other sights of their island.

And the pushmi-pullyu was glad they had come; because he liked the green grass so much better than the dried apples he had been eating on the ship. And Gub-Gub squeaked for joy when he found a whole valley full of wild sugar-cane.

A little later, when they had all had plenty

to eat and drink, and were lying on their backs while the canaries sang for them, two of the swallows came hurrying up, very flustered and excited.

"Doctor!" they cried, "the pirates have come into the bay; and they've all got on to your ship. They are downstairs looking for things to steal. They have left their own ship with nobody on it. If you hurry and come down to the shore, you can get on to their ship—which is very fast—and escape. But you'll have to hurry."

"That's a good idea," said the Doctor—"splendid!"

And he called his animals together at once, said good-by to the canaries and ran down to the beach.

When they reached the shore they saw the pirate-ship, with the three red sails, standing in the water; and—just as the swallows had said—there was nobody on it; all the pirates were downstairs in the Doctor's ship, looking for things to steal.

So John Dolittle told his animals to walk very softly and they all crept on to the pirate-ship.

THE FIFTEENTH CHAPTER

THE BARBARY DRAGON

EVERYTHING would have gone all right if the pig had not caught a cold in his head while eating the damp sugar-cane on the island. This is what happened: After they had pulled up the anchor without a sound, and were moving the ship very, very carefully out of the bay, Gub-Gub suddenly sneezed so loud that the pirates on the other ship came rushing upstairs to see what the noise was.

As soon as they saw that the Doctor was escaping, they sailed the other boat right across the entrance to the bay so that the Doctor could not get out into the open sea.

Then the leader of these bad men (who called himself "Ben Ali, The Dragon") shook his fist at the Doctor and shouted across the water, "Ha!

Ha! You are caught, my fine friend! You were going to run off in my ship, eh? But you are not a good enough sailor to beat Ben Ali, the Barbary Dragon. I want that duck you've got—and the pig too. We'll have pork-chops and roast duck for supper tonight. And before I let you go home, you must make your friends send me a trunk-full of gold."

Poor Gub-Gub began to weep; and Dab-Dab made ready to fly to save her life. But the owl, Too-Too, whispered to the Doctor, "Keep him talking, Doctor. Be pleasant to him. Our old ship is bound to sink soon—the rats said it would be at the bottom of the sea before tomorrow night—and the rats are never wrong. Be pleasant, till the ship sinks under him. Keep him talking."

"What, until tomorrow night!" said the Doctor. "Well, I'll do my best. . . . Let me see—what shall I talk about?"

"Oh, let them come on," said Jip. "We can fight the dirty rascals. There are only six of them. Let them come on. I'd love to tell that collie next door, when we get home, that I had bitten a real pirate. Let 'em come. We can fight them."

" 'Look here, Ben Ali—' "

"But they have pistols and swords," said the Doctor. "No, that would never do. I must talk to him. . . . Look here, Ben Ali—"

But before the Doctor could say any more, the pirates began to sail the ship nearer, laughing with glee, and saying one to another, "Who shall be the first to catch the pig?"

Poor Gub-Gub was dreadfully frightened; and the pushmi-pullyu began to sharpen his horns for a fight by rubbing them on the mast of the ship; while Jip kept springing into the air and barking and calling Ben Ali bad names in dog-language.

But presently something seemed to go wrong with the pirates; they stopped laughing and cracking jokes; they looked puzzled; something was making them uneasy.

Then Ben Ali, staring down at his feet, suddenly bellowed out, "Thunder and Lightning!—Men, *the boat's leaking!*"

And then the other pirates peered over the side and they saw that the boat was indeed getting lower and lower in the water. And one of them said to Ben Ali, "But surely if this old boat were sinking we should see the rats leaving it."

And Jip shouted across from the other ship, "You great duffers, there are no rats there to leave! They left two hours ago! 'Ha, ha,' to you, 'my fine friends!' "

But of course the men did not understand him.

Soon the front end of the ship began to go down and down, faster and faster—till the boat looked almost as though it were standing on its head; and the pirates had to cling to the rails and the masts and the ropes and anything to keep from sliding off. Then the sea rushed roaring in through all the windows and the doors. And at last the ship plunged right down to the bottom of the sea, making a dreadful gurgling sound; and the six bad men were left bobbing about in the deep water of the bay.

Some of them started to swim for the shores of the island; while others came and tried to get on to the boat where the Doctor was. But Jip kept snapping at their noses, so they were afraid to climb up the side of the ship.

Then suddenly they all cried out in great fear, "*The sharks!* The sharks are coming! Let us get on to the ship before they eat us! Help, help!—The sharks! The sharks!"

And now the Doctor could see, all over the bay, the backs of big fishes swimming swiftly through the water.

And one great shark came near to the ship, and poking his nose out of the water he said to the Doctor, "Are you John Dolittle, the famous animal-doctor?"

"Yes," said Doctor Dolittle. "That is my name."

"Well," said the shark, "we know these pirates to be a bad lot—especially Ben Ali. If they are annoying you, we will gladly eat them up for you—and then you won't be troubled any more."

"Thank you," said the Doctor. "This is really most attentive. But I don't think it will be necessary to eat them. Don't let any of them reach the shore until I tell you—just keep them swimming about, will you? And please make Ben Ali swim over here that I may talk to him."

So the shark went off and chased Ben Ali over to the Doctor.

"Listen, Ben Ali," said John Dolittle, leaning over the side. "You have been a very bad man; and I understand that you have killed many people. These good sharks here have just offered to eat you up for me—and 'twould indeed be a good thing if the seas were rid of you. But if you will promise to do as I tell you, I will let you go in safety."

"What must I do?" asked the pirate, looking down sideways at the big shark who was smelling his leg under the water.

"You must kill no more people," said the Doctor; "you must stop stealing; you must never sink another ship; you must give up being a pirate altogether."

"But what shall I do then?" asked Ben Ali.

"How shall I live?"

"You and all your men must go on to this island and be bird-seed-farmers," the Doctor answered. "You must grow bird-seed for the canaries."

The Barbary Dragon turned pale with anger, "*Grow bird-seed!*" he groaned in disgust. "Can't I be a sailor?"

"No," said the Doctor, "you cannot. You have been a sailor long enough—and sent many stout ships and good men to the bottom of the sea. For the rest of your life you must be a peaceful farmer. The shark is waiting. Do not waste any more of his time. Make up your mind."

"Thunder and Lightning!" Ben Ali muttered—"*Bird-seed!*" Then he looked down into the water again and saw the great fish smelling his other leg.

"Very well," he said sadly. "We'll be farmers."

"And remember," said the Doctor, "that if you do not keep your promise—if you start killing and stealing again, I shall hear of it, because the canaries will come and tell me. And be very sure that I will find a way to punish you. For though I may not be able to sail a ship as well as you, so long as the birds and the beasts and the fishes are my friends, I do not have to be afraid of a pirate chief—even though he call himself 'The Dragon of Barbary.' Now go and be a good farmer and live in peace."

Then the Doctor turned to the big shark, and waving his hand he said, "All right. Let them swim safely to the land."

THE SIXTEENTH CHAPTER
TOO-TOO, THE LISTENER

HAVING thanked the sharks again for their kindness, the Doctor and his pets set off once more on their journey home in the swift ship with the three red sails.

As they moved out into the open sea, the animals all went downstairs to see what their new boat was like inside; while the Doctor leant on the rail at the back of the ship with a pipe in his mouth, watching the Canary Islands fade away in the blue dusk of the evening.

While he was standing there, wondering how the monkeys were getting on—and what his garden would look like when he got back to Puddleby, Dab-Dab came tumbling up the stairs, all smiles and full of news.

"Doctor!" she cried. "This ship of the pirates

is simply beautiful—absolutely. The beds downstairs are made of primrose silk—with hundreds of big pillows and cushions; there are thick, soft carpets on the floors; the dishes are made of silver; and there are all sorts of good things to eat and drink—special things; the larder—well, it's just like a shop, that's all. You never saw anything like it in your life—Just think—they kept five different kinds of sardines, those men! Come and look. . . . Oh, and we found a little room down there with the door locked; and we are all crazy to get in and see what's inside. Jip says it must be where the pirates kept their treasure. But we can't open the door. Come down and see if you can let us in."

So the Doctor went downstairs and he saw that it was indeed a beautiful ship. He found the animals gathered round a little door, all talking at once, trying to guess what was inside. The Doctor turned the handle but it wouldn't open. Then they all started to hunt for the key. They looked under the mat; they looked under all the carpets; they looked in all the cupboards and drawers and lockers—in the big chests in the ship's dining-room; they looked everywhere.

While they were doing this they discovered

a lot of new and wonderful things that the pirates must have stolen from other ships: Kashmir shawls as thin as a cobweb, embroidered with flowers of gold; jars of fine tobacco from Jamaica; carved ivory boxes full of Russian tea; an old violin with a string broken and a picture on the back; a set of big chess-men, carved out of coral and amber; a walking-stick which had a sword inside it when you pulled the handle; six wine-glasses with turquoise and silver round the rims; and a lovely great sugar-bowl, made of mother o' pearl. But nowhere in the whole boat could they find a key to fit that lock.

So they all came back to the door, and Jip peered through the key-hole. But something had been stood against the wall on the inside and he could see nothing.

While they were standing around, wondering what they should do, the owl, Too-Too, suddenly said, "Sh!—Listen!—I do believe there's someone in there!"

They all kept still a moment. Then the Doctor said, "You must be mistaken, Too-Too. I don't hear anything."

"I'm sure of it," said the owl. "Sh!—There it is again—don't you hear that?"

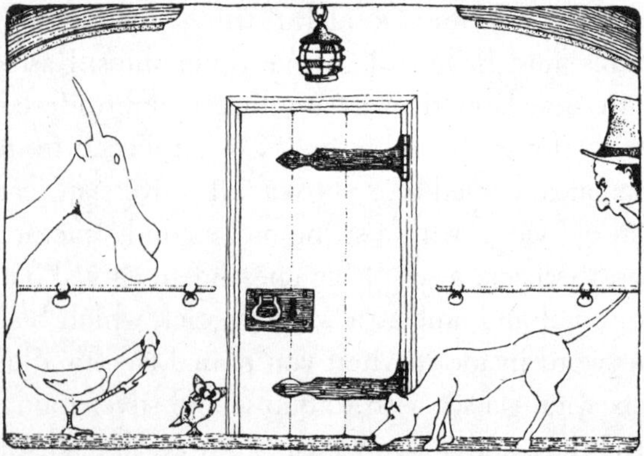

" 'Sh!—Listen!—I do believe there's someone in there!' "

"No, I do not," said the Doctor. "What kind of a sound is it?"

"I hear the noise of some one putting his hand in his pocket," said the owl.

"But that makes hardly any sound at all," said the Doctor. "You couldn't hear that out here."

"Pardon me, but I can," said Too-Too. "I tell you there is someone on the other side of that door putting his hand in his pocket. Almost everything makes *some* noise—if your ears are only sharp enough to catch it. Bats can hear a mole walking in his tunnel under the earth—and they think they're good hearers. But we owls can tell you, using only one ear, the color of a kitten from the way it winks in the dark."

"Well, well!" said the Doctor. "You surprise me. That's very interesting. . . . Listen again and tell me what he's doing now."

"I'm not sure yet," said Too-Too, "if it's a man at all. Maybe it's a woman. Lift me up and let me listen at the key-hole and I'll soon tell you."

So the Doctor lifted the owl up and held him close to the lock of the door.

After a moment Too-Too said, "Now he's rubbing his face with his left hand. It is a small hand and a small face. It *might* be a woman—no. Now he pushes his hair back off his forehead—it's a man all right."

"Women sometimes do that," said the Doctor.

"True," said the owl. "But when they do, their long hair makes quite a different sound. . . . Sh! Make that fidgety pig keep still. Now all hold your breath a moment so I can listen well. This is very difficult, what I'm doing now—and the pesky door is so thick! Sh! Everybody quite still—shut your eyes and don't breathe."

Too-Too leaned down and listened again very hard and long.

At last he looked up into the Doctor's face

and said, "The man in there is unhappy. He weeps. He has taken care not to blubber or snifle, lest we should find out that he is crying. But I heard—quite distinctly—the sound of a tear falling on his sleeve."

"How do you know it wasn't a drop of water falling off the ceiling on him?" asked Gub-Gub.

"Pshaw!—Such ignorance!" sniffed Too-Too. "A drop of water falling off the ceiling would have made ten times as much noise!"

"Well," said the Doctor, "if the poor fellow's unhappy, we've got to get in and see what's the matter with him. Find me an axe, and I'll chop the door down."

THE SEVENTEENTH CHAPTER

THE OCEAN GOSSIPS

RIGHT away an axe was found. And the Doctor soon chopped a hole in the door big enough to clamber through.

At first he could see nothing at all, it was so dark inside. So he struck a match.

The room was quite small; no window; the ceiling, low. For furniture there was only one little stool. All round the room big barrels stood against the walls, fastened at the bottom so they wouldn't tumble with the rolling of the ship; and above the barrels, pewter jugs of all sizes hung from wooden pegs. There was a strong, winey smell. And in the middle of the floor sat a little boy, about eight years old, crying bitterly.

"I declare, it is the pirates' rum-room!" said Jip in a whisper.

"Yes. Very rum!" said Gub-Gub. "The smell makes me giddy."

The little boy seemed rather frightened to find a man standing there before him and all those animals staring in through the hole in the broken door. But as soon as he saw John Dolittle's face by the light of the match, he stopped crying and got up.

"You aren't one of the pirates, are you?" he asked.

And when the Doctor threw back his head and laughed long and loud, the little boy smiled too and came and took his hand.

"You laugh like a friend," he said—"not like a pirate. Could you tell me where my uncle is?"

"I am afraid I can't," said the Doctor. "When did you see him last?"

"It was the day before yesterday," said the boy. "I and my uncle were out fishing in our little boat, when the pirates came and caught us. They sunk our fishing-boat and brought us both on to this ship. They told my uncle that they wanted him to be a pirate like them—for he was clever at sailing a ship in all weathers. But he said he didn't want to be a pirate, because killing people and stealing was no work for a good fisherman to do. Then the leader, Ben Ali, got very angry and gnashed his teeth, and said they would throw my uncle into the sea if he didn't do as they said. They sent me downstairs; and I heard the noise of a fight going on above. And when they let me come up again next day, my uncle was nowhere to be seen. I asked the pirates where he was; but they wouldn't tell me. I am very much afraid they threw him into the sea and drowned him."

And the little boy began to cry again.

"Well now—wait a minute," said the Doctor. "Don't cry. Let's go and have tea in the dining room, and we'll talk it over. Maybe your uncle is quite safe all the time. You don't *know* that he was drowned, do you? And that's something. Perhaps we can find him for you. First we'll go and have tea—with strawberry-jam; and then we will see what can be done."

All the animals had been standing around listening with great curiosity. And when they had gone into the ship's dining-room and were having tea, Dab-Dab came up behind the Doctor's chair and whispered, "Ask the porpoises if the boy's uncle was drowned—they'll know."

"All right," said the Doctor, taking a second

piece of bread-and-jam.

"What are those funny, clicking noises you are making with your tongue?" asked the boy.

"Oh, I just said a couple of words in duck-language," the Doctor answered. "This is Dab-Dab, one of my pets."

"I didn't even know that ducks had a language," said the boy. "Are all these other animals your pets, too? What is that strange-looking thing with two heads?"

"Sh!" the Doctor whispered. "That is the pushmi-pullyu. Don't let him see we're talking about him—he gets so dreadfully embarrassed. . . . Tell me, how did you come to be locked up in that little room?"

"The pirates shut me in there when they were going off to steal things from another ship. When I heard some one chopping on the door, I didn't know who it could be. I was very glad to find it was you. Do you think you will be able to find my uncle for me?"

"Well, we are going to try very hard," said the Doctor. "Now what was your uncle like to look at?"

"He had red hair," the boy answered—"very red hair, and the picture of an anchor tattooed on his arm. He was a strong man, a kind uncle and the best sailor in the South Atlantic. His fishing-boat was called *The Saucy Sally*—a cutter-rigged sloop."

"What's 'cutterigsloop'?" whispered Gub-Gub, turning to Jip.

"Sh!—That's the kind of a ship the man had," said Jip. "Keep still, can't you?"

"Oh," said the pig, "is that all? I thought it was something to drink."

So the Doctor left the boy to play with the animals in the dining-room, and went upstairs to look for passing porpoises.

And soon a whole school came dancing and jumping through the water, on their way to Brazil.

When they saw the Doctor leaning on the rail of his ship, they came over to see how he was getting on.

And the Doctor asked them if they had seen anything of a man with red hair and an anchor tattooed on his arm.

"Do you mean the master of *The Saucy Sally*?" asked the porpoises.

"Yes," said the Doctor. "That's the man. Has he been drowned?"

"His fishing-sloop was sunk," said the porpoises—"for we saw it lying on the bottom of the sea. But there was nobody inside it, because we went and looked."

"His little nephew is on the ship with me here," said the Doctor. "And he is terribly afraid that the pirates threw his uncle into the sea. Would you be so good as to find out for me, for sure, whether he has been drowned or not?"

"Oh, he isn't drowned," said the porpoises. "If he were, we would be sure to have heard of it from the deep-sea Decapods. We hear all the salt-water news. The shell-fish call us 'The Ocean Gossips.' No—tell the little boy we are sorry we do not know where his uncle is; but we are quite certain he hasn't been drowned in the sea."

So the Doctor ran downstairs with the news and told the nephew, who clapped his hands with happiness. And the pushmi-pullyu took the little boy on his back and gave him a ride round the dining-room table; while all the other animals followed behind, beating the dish-covers with spoons, pretending it was a parade.

THE EIGHTEENTH CHAPTER
SMELLS

"YOUR uncle must now be *found*," said the Doctor—"that is the next thing—now that we know he wasn't thrown into the sea."

Then Dab-Dab came up to him again and whispered, "Ask the eagles to look for the man. No living creature can see better than an eagle. When they are miles high in the air they can count the ants crawling on the ground. Ask the eagles."

So the Doctor sent one of the swallows off to get some eagles.

And in about an hour the little bird came back with six different kinds of eagles: a Black Eagle, a Bald Eagle, a Fish Eagle, a Golden Eagle, an Eagle-Vulture, and a White-tailed Sea Eagle. Twice as high as the boy they were, each one of them. And they stood on the rail of the ship, like round-shouldered soldiers all in a row, stern and still and stiff; while their great, gleaming, black eyes shot darting glances here and there and everywhere.

Gub-Gub was scared of them and got behind a barrel. He said he felt as though those terrible eyes were looking right inside of him to see what he had stolen for lunch.

And the Doctor said to the eagles, "A man has been lost—a fisherman with red hair and an anchor marked on his arm. Would you be so kind as to see if you can find him for us? This boy is the man's nephew."

Eagles do not talk very much. And all they answered in their husky voices was, "You may be sure that we will do our best—for John Dolittle."

Then they flew off—and Gub-Gub came out from behind his barrel to see them go. Up and up and up they went—higher and higher and higher still. Then, when the Doctor could only just see them, they parted company and started going off all different ways—North, East, South and West, looking like tiny grains of black sand creeping across the wide, blue sky.

"My gracious!" said Gub-Gub in a hushed

voice. "What a height! I wonder they don't scorch their feathers—so near the sun!"

They were gone a long time. And when they came back it was almost night.

And the eagles said to the Doctor, "We have searched all the seas and all the countries and all the islands and all the cities and all the villages in this half of the world. But we have failed. In the main street of Gibraltar we saw three red hairs lying on a wheelbarrow before a baker's door. But they were not the hairs of a man—they were the hairs out of a fur-coat. Nowhere, on land or water, could we see any sign of this boy's uncle. And if *we* could not see him, then he is not to be seen. . . . For John Dolittle—we have done our best."

Then the six great birds flapped their big wings and flew back to their homes in the mountains and the rocks.

"Well," said Dab-Dab, after they had gone, "what are we going to do now? The boy's uncle *must* be found—there's no two ways about that. The lad isn't old enough to be knocking around the world by himself. Boys aren't like duck-lings—they have to be taken care of till they're quite old. . . . I wish Chee-Chee were here. He would soon find the man. Good old Chee-Chee! I wonder how he's getting on!"

"If we only had Polynesia with us," said the white mouse. "*She* would soon think of some way. Do you remember how she got us all out of prison—the second time? My, but she was a clever one!"

"I don't think so much of those eagle-fellows," said Jip. "They're just conceited. They may have very good eyesight and all that; but when you ask them to find a man for you, they can't do it—and they have the cheek to come back and say that nobody else could do it. They're just conceited—like that collie in Puddleby. And I don't think a whole lot of those gossipy old porpoises either. All they could tell us was that the man isn't in the sea. We don't want to know where he *isn't*—we want to know where he *is*."

"Oh, don't talk so much," said Gub-Gub. "It's easy to talk; but it isn't so easy to find a man when you have got the whole world to hunt him in. Maybe the fisherman's hair has turned white, worrying about the boy; and that was why the eagles didn't find him. You don't know everything. You're just talking. You are not doing anything to help.

You couldn't find the boy's uncle any more than the eagles could—you couldn't do as well."

"Couldn't I?" said the dog. "That's all you know, you stupid piece of warm bacon! I haven't begun to try yet, have I? You wait and see!"

" 'You stupid piece of warm bacon!' "

Then Jip went to the Doctor and said, "Ask the boy if he has anything in his pockets that belonged to his uncle, will you, please?"

So the Doctor asked him. And the boy showed them a gold ring which he wore on a piece of string around his neck because it was too big for his finger. He said his uncle gave it to him when they saw the pirates coming.

Jip smelt the ring and said, "That's no good. Ask him if he has anything else that belonged to his uncle."

Then the boy took from his pocket a great, big red handkerchief and said, "This was my uncle's too."

As soon as the boy pulled it out, Jip shouted, "*Snuff*, by Jingo!—Black Rappee snuff. Don't you smell it? His uncle took snuff—ask him, Doctor."

The Doctor questioned the boy again; and he said, "Yes. My uncle took a lot of snuff."

"Fine!" said Jip. "The man's as good as found. 'Twill be as easy as stealing milk from a kitten. Tell the boy I'll find his uncle for him in less than a week. Let us go upstairs and see which way the wind is blowing."

"But it is dark now," said the Doctor. "You can't find him in the dark!"

"I don't need any light to look for a man who smells of Black Rappee snuff," said Jip as he climbed the stairs. "If the man had a hard smell, like string, now—or hot water, it would be different. But *snuff!*—Tut, tut!"

"Does hot water have a smell?" asked the Doctor.

"Certainly it has," said Jip. "Hot water smells quite different from cold water. It is warm water—or ice—that has the really difficult smell. Why, I once followed a man for ten miles on a dark night by the smell of the hot water he had used to shave with—for the poor fellow had no soap. . . . Now then, let us see which way the wind is blowing. Wind is very important in long-distant smelling. It mustn't be too fierce a wind—and of course it must blow the right way. A nice, steady, damp breeze is the best of all. . . . Ha!—This wind is from the North."

Then Jip went up to the front of the ship and smelt the wind; and he started muttering to himself, "Tar; Spanish onions; kerosene oil; wet raincoats; crushed laurel-leaves; rubber burning; lace-curtains being washed—No, my mistake, lace-curtains hanging out to dry; and foxes—hundreds of 'em—cubs; and—"

"Can you really smell all those different things in this one wind?" asked the Doctor.

"Why, of course!" said Jip. "And those are only a few of the easy smells—the strong ones.

Any mongrel could smell those with a cold in the head. Wait now, and I'll tell you some of the harder scents that are coming on this wind—a few of the dainty ones."

Then the dog shut his eyes tight, poked his nose straight up in the air and sniffed hard with his mouth half-open.

For a long time he said nothing. He kept as still as a stone. He hardly seemed to be breathing at all. When at last he began to speak, it sounded almost as though he were singing, sadly, in a dream.

"Bricks," he whispered, very low—"old yellow bricks, crumbling with age in a garden-wall; the sweet breath of young cows standing in a mountain-stream; the lead roof of a dove-cote—or perhaps a granary—with the mid-day sun on it; black kid gloves lying in a bureau-drawer of walnut-wood; a dusty road with a horses' drinking-trough beneath the sycamores; little mushrooms bursting through the rotting leaves; and—and—and—"

"Any parsnips?" asked Gub-Gub.

"No," said Jip. "You always think of things to eat. No parsnips whatever. And no snuff—plenty of pipes and cigarettes, and a few cigars. But no snuff. We must wait till the wind changes to the South."

"Yes, it's a poor wind, that," said Gub-Gub. "I think you're a fake, Jip. Who ever heard of finding a man in the middle of the ocean just by smell! I told you you couldn't do it."

"Look here," said Jip, getting really angry. "You're going to get a bite on the nose in a minute! You needn't think that just because the Doctor won't let us give you what you deserve, that you can be as cheeky as you like!"

"Stop quarreling!" said the Doctor—"Stop it! Life's too short. Tell me, Jip, where do you think those smells are coming from?"

"From Devon and Wales—most of them," said Jip—"The wind is coming that way."

"Well, well!" said the Doctor. "You know that's really quite remarkable—quite. I must make a note of that for my new book. I wonder if you could train me to smell as well as that. . . . But no—perhaps I'm better off the way I am. 'Enough is as good as a feast,' they say. Let's go down to supper. I'm quite hungry."

"So am I," said Gub-Gub.

THE NINETEENTH CHAPTER

THE ROCK

UP they got, early next morning, out of the silken beds; and they saw that the sun was shining brightly and that the wind was blowing from the South.

Jip smelt the South wind for half an hour. Then he came to the Doctor, shaking his head.

"I smell no snuff as yet," he said. "We must wait till the wind changes to the East."

But even when the East wind came, at three o'clock that afternoon, the dog could not catch the smell of snuff.

The little boy was terribly disappointed and began to cry again, saying that no one seemed to be able to find his uncle for him. But all Jip said to the Doctor was, "Tell him that when the wind changes to the West, I'll find his uncle even though he be in China—so long as he is still taking Black Rappee snuff."

Three days they had to wait before the West wind came. This was on a Friday morning, early—just as it was getting light. A fine rainy mist lay on the sea like a thin fog. And the wind was soft and warm and wet.

As soon as Jip awoke he ran upstairs and poked his nose in the air. Then he got most frightfully excited and rushed down again to wake the Doctor up.

"Doctor!" he cried. "I've got it! Doctor! Doctor! Wake up! Listen! I've got it! The wind's from the West and it smells of nothing but snuff. Come upstairs and start the ship—quick!"

So the Doctor tumbled out of bed and went to the rudder to steer the ship.

"Now I'll go up to the front," said Jip; "and you watch my nose—whichever way I point it, you turn the ship the same way. The man cannot be far off—with the smell as strong as this. And the wind's all lovely and wet. Now watch me!"

So all that morning Jip stood in the front part of the ship, sniffing the wind and pointing the way for the Doctor to steer; while all the ani-

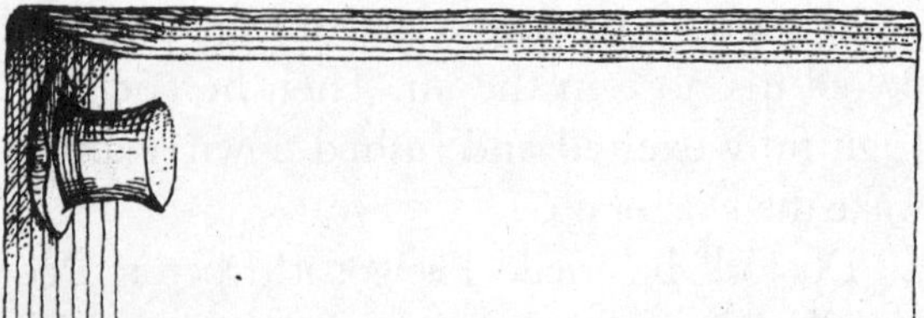

" 'Doctor!' he cried. 'I've got it!' "

mals and the little boy stood round with their eyes wide open, watching the dog in wonder.

About lunch-time Jip asked Dab-Dab to tell the Doctor that he was getting worried and wanted to speak to him. So Dab-Dab went and fetched the Doctor from the other end of the ship and Jip said to him, "The boy's uncle is starving. We must make the ship go as fast as we can."

"How do you know he is starving?" asked the Doctor.

"Because there is no other smell in the West wind but snuff," said Jip. "If the man were cooking or eating food of any kind, I would be bound to smell it too. But he hasn't even fresh water to drink. All he is taking is snuff—in large pinches. We are getting nearer to him all the time, because the smell grows stronger every minute. But make the ship go as fast as you can, for I am certain that the man is starving."

"All right," said the Doctor; and he sent Dab-Dab to ask the swallows to pull the ship, the same as they had done when the pirates were chasing them.

So the stout little birds came down and once more harnessed themselves to the ship.

And now the boat went bounding through the waves at a terrible speed. It went so fast that the fishes in the sea had to jump for their lives to get out of the way and not be run over.

And all the animals got tremendously excited; and they gave up looking at Jip and turned to watch the sea in front, to spy out any land or islands where the starving man might be.

But hour after hour went by and still the ship went rushing on, over the same flat, flat sea; and no land anywhere came in sight.

And now the animals gave up chattering and sat around silent, anxious and miserable. The little boy again grew sad. And on Jip's face there was a worried look.

At last, late in the afternoon, just as the sun was going down, the owl, Too-Too, who was perched on the tip of the mast, suddenly startled them all by crying out at the top of his voice, "Jip! Jip! I see a great, great rock in front of us—look—way out there where the sky and the water meet. See the sun shine on it—like gold! Is the smell coming from there?"

And Jip called back, "Yes. That's it. That is where the man is.—At last, at last!"

And when they got nearer they could see that

the rock was very large—as large as a big field. No trees grew on it, no grass—nothing. The great rock was as smooth and as bare as the back of a tortoise.

Then the Doctor sailed the ship right round the rock. But nowhere on it could a man be seen. All the animals screwed up their eyes and looked as hard as they could; and John Dolittle got a telescope from downstairs.

But not one living thing could they spy—not even a gull, nor a star-fish, nor a shred of sea-weed.

They all stood still and listened, straining their ears for any sound. But the only noise they heard was the gentle lapping of the little waves against the sides of their ship.

Then they all started calling, "Hulloa, there!—HULLOA!" till their voices were hoarse. But only the echo came back from the rock.

And the little boy burst into tears and said, "I am afraid I shall never see my uncle any more! What shall I tell them when I get home!"

But Jip called to the Doctor, "He must be there—he must—*he must!* The smell goes on no further. He must be there, I tell you! Sail the ship close to the rock and let me jump out on it."

So the Doctor brought the ship as close as he could and let down the anchor. Then he and Jip got out of the ship on to the rock.

Jip at once put his nose down close to the ground and began to run all over the place. Up and down he went, back and forth—zig-zagging, twisting, doubling and turning. And everywhere he went, the Doctor ran behind him, close at his heels—till he was terribly out of breath.

At last Jip let out a great bark and sat down. And when the Doctor came running up to him, he found the dog staring into a big, deep hole in the middle of the rock.

"The boy's uncle is down there," said Jip quietly. "No wonder those silly eagles couldn't see him!—It takes a dog to find a man."

So the Doctor got down into the hole, which seemed to be a kind of cave, or tunnel, running a long way under the ground. Then he struck a match and started to make his way along the dark passage with Jip following behind.

The Doctor's match soon went out; and he had to strike another and another and another.

At last the passage came to an end; and the

Doctor found himself in a kind of tiny room with walls of rock.

And there, in the middle of the room, his head resting on his arms, lay a man with very red hair—fast asleep!

Jip went up and sniffed at something lying on the ground beside him. The Doctor stooped and picked it up. It was an enormous snuff-box. And it was full of Black Rappee!

THE TWENTIETH CHAPTER

THE FISHERMAN'S TOWN

GENTLY then—very gently, the Doctor woke the man up.

But just at that moment the match went out again. And the man thought it was Ben Ali coming back, and he began to punch the Doctor in the dark.

But when John Dolittle told him who it was, and that he had his little nephew safe on his ship, the man was tremendously glad, and said he was sorry he had fought the Doctor. He had not hurt him much though—because it was too dark to punch properly. Then he gave the Doctor a pinch of snuff.

And the man told how the Barbary Dragon had put him on to this rock and left him there, when he wouldn't promise to become a pirate;

and how he used to sleep down in this hole because there was no house on the rock to keep him warm.

And then he said, "For four days I have had nothing to eat or drink. I have lived on snuff."

"There you are!" said Jip. "What did I tell you?"

So they struck some more matches and made their way out through the passage into the daylight; and the Doctor hurried the man down to the boat to get some soup.

When the animals and the little boy saw the Doctor and Jip coming back to the ship with a red-headed man, they began to cheer and yell and dance about the boat. And the swallows up above started whistling at the top of their voices—thousands and millions of them—to show that they too were glad that the boy's brave uncle had been found. The noise they made was so great that sailors far out at sea thought that a terrible storm was coming. "Hark to that gale howling in the East!" they said.

And Jip was awfully proud of himself—though he tried hard not to look conceited. When Dab-Dab came to him and said, "Jip, I had no idea you were so clever!" he just tossed his head and answered, "Oh, that's nothing special. But it takes a dog to find a man, you know. Birds are no good for a game like that."

Then the Doctor asked the red-haired fisherman where his home was. And when he had told him, the Doctor asked the swallows to guide the ship there first.

And when they had come to the land which the man had spoken of, they saw a little fishing-town at the foot of a rocky mountain; and the man pointed out the house where he lived.

And while they were letting down the anchor, the little boy's mother (who was also the man's sister) came running down to the shore to meet them, laughing and crying at the same time. She had been sitting on a hill for twenty days, watching the sea and waiting for them to return.

And she kissed the Doctor many times, so that he giggled and blushed like a school-girl. And she tried to kiss Jip too; but he ran away and hid inside the ship.

"It's a silly business, this kissing," he said. "I don't hold by it. Let her go and kiss Gub-Gub—if she *must* kiss something."

The fisherman and his sister didn't want the

Doctor to go away again in a hurry. They begged him to spend a few days with them. So John Dolittle and his animals had to stay at their house a whole Saturday and Sunday and half of Monday.

And all the little boys of the fishing-village went down to the beach and pointed at the great ship anchored there, and said to one another in whispers, "Look! That was a pirate-ship—Ben Ali's—the most terrible pirate that ever sailed the Seven Seas! That old gentleman with the high hat, who's staying up at Mrs. Trevelyan's, *he* took the ship away from The Barbary Dragon—and made him into a farmer. Who'd have thought it of him—him so gentle-like and all! . . . Look at the great red sails! Ain't she the wicked looking ship—and fast?—My!"

All those two days and a half that the Doctor stayed at the little fishing-town the people kept asking him out to teas and luncheons and dinners and parties; all the ladies sent him boxes of flowers and candies; and the village-band played tunes under his window every night.

At last the Doctor said, "Good people, I must go home now. You have really been most kind. I shall always remember it. But I must go home—for I have things to do."

Then, just as the Doctor was about to leave, the Mayor of the town came down the street and a lot of other people in grand clothes with him. And the Mayor stopped before the house where the Doctor was living; and everybody in the village gathered round to see what was going to happen.

After six page-boys had blown on shining trumpets to make the people stop talking, the Doctor came out on to the steps and the Mayor spoke.

"Doctor John Dolittle," said he: "It is a great pleasure for me to present to the man who rid the seas of the Dragon of Barbary this little token from the grateful people of our worthy Town."

And the Mayor took from his pocket a little tissue-paper packet, and opening it, he handed to the Doctor a perfectly beautiful watch with real diamonds in the back.

Then the Mayor pulled out of his pocket a still larger parcel and said, "Where is the dog?"

Then everybody started to hunt for Jip. And at last Dab-Dab found him on the other side of the village in a stable-yard, where all the dogs of the country-side were standing round him speechless with admiration and respect.

When Jip was brought to the Doctor's side, the Mayor opened the larger parcel; and inside was a dog-collar made of solid gold! And a great murmur of wonder went up from the village-folk as the Mayor bent down and fastened it round the dog's neck with his own hands.

For written on the collar in big letters were these words: "JIP—*The Cleverest Dog in the World.*"

Then the whole crowd moved down to the beach to see them off. And after the red-haired fisherman and his sister and the little boy had thanked the Doctor and his dog over and over and over again, the great, swift ship with the red sails was turned once more towards Puddleby and they sailed out to sea, while the village-band played music on the shore.

THE LAST CHAPTER
HOME AGAIN

MARCH winds had come and gone; April's showers were over; May's buds had opened into flower; and the June sun was shining on the pleasant fields, when John Dolittle at last got back to his own country.

But he did not yet go home to Puddleby. First he went traveling through the land with the pushmi-pullyu in a gipsy-wagon, stopping at all the country-fairs. And there, with the acrobats on one side of them and the Punch-and-Judy show on the other, they would hang out a big sign which read, "COME AND SEE THE MARVELOUS TWO-HEADED ANIMAL FROM THE JUNGLES OF AFRICA. Admission SIXPENCE."

And the pushmi-pullyu would stay inside the

wagon, while the other animals would lie about underneath. The Doctor sat in a chair in front taking the sixpences and smiling on the people as they went in; and Dab-Dab was kept busy all the time scolding him because he would let the children in for nothing when she wasn't looking.

And menagerie-keepers and circus-men came and asked the Doctor to sell them the strange creature, saying they would pay a tremendous lot of money for him. But the Doctor always shook his head and said, "No. The pushmi-pullyu shall never be shut up in a cage. He shall be free always to come and go, like you and me."

Many curious sights and happenings they saw in this wandering life; but they all seemed quite ordinary after the great things they had seen and done in foreign lands. It was very interesting at first, being sort of part of a circus; but after a few weeks they all got dreadfully tired of it and the Doctor and all of them were longing to go home.

But so many people came flocking to the little wagon and paid the sixpence to go inside and see the pushmi-pullyu that very soon the Doctor was able to give up being a showman.

"The Doctor sat in a chair in front"

And one fine day, when the hollyhocks were in full bloom, he came back to Puddleby a rich man, to live in the little house with the big garden.

And the old lame horse in the stable was glad to see him; and so were the swallows who had already built their nests under the eaves of his roof and had young ones. And Dab-Dab was glad, too, to get back to the house she knew so well—although there was a terrible lot of dusting to be done, with cobwebs everywhere.

And after Jip had gone and shown his golden collar to the conceited collie next-door, he came back and began running round the garden like a crazy thing, looking for the bones he had buried long ago, and chasing the rats out of the toolshed; while Gub-Gub dug up the horseradish which had grown three feet high in the corner by the garden wall.

And the Doctor went and saw the sailor who had lent him the boat, and he bought two new ships for him and a rubber-doll for his baby; and he paid the grocer for the food he had lent him for the journey to Africa. And he bought another piano and put the white mice back in it—because they said the bureau-drawer was drafty.

"He began running round the garden like a crazy thing"

Even when the Doctor had filled the old money-box on the dresser-shelf, he still had a lot of money left; and he had to get three more money-boxes, just as big, to put the rest in.

"Money," he said, "is a terrible nuisance. But it's nice not to have to worry."

"Yes," said Dab-Dab, who was toasting muffins for his tea, "it is indeed!"

And when the winter came again, and the snow flew against the kitchen-window, the Doctor and his animals would sit round the big, warm fire after supper; and he would read aloud to them out of his books.

But far away in Africa, where the monkeys chattered in the palm-trees before they went to bed under the big yellow moon, they would say to one another, "I wonder what The Good Man's doing now—over there, in the Land Across the Ocean! Do you think he ever will come back?"

And Polynesia would squeak out from the vines, "I think he will—I guess he will—I hope he will!"

And then the crocodile would grunt up at them from the black mud of the river, "I'm SURE he will—Go to sleep!"

THE EN
ROSES

Notes

The First Chapter
PUDDLEBY

p.7 4 M.D. (Medicinae Doctor) 医学博士　7 knew him well by sight 彼の顔をよく知っていた　13 caw カーカーと鳴く

p.9 2 weeping-willows シダレヤナギ　4 looked after . . . ～の世話をした　8 pantry 食料品置き場　9 hedgehog ハリネズミ　10 calf 子牛　10 lame 足が不自由な　16 grumble 文句を言う　17 untidy 散らかった　18 rheumatism リューマチ

p.10 3 personage 人物　4 Squire 地方地主　4 Parson 教区牧師　11 ridiculous ばかばかしい　16 Cat's-meat-Man 猫肉屋（ペットの猫に食べさせる屑肉を売り歩く業者）　20 sixpence 6ペンス銀貨（「ペンス」は「ペニー(penny)」の複数形）

p.12 4 bureau-drawer タンスの引き出し

The Second Chapter
ANIMAL LANGUAGE

p.13 3 stomachache 胃痛　13 vets (veterinarians) 獣医　16 scholar 学者

p.14 13 make them droopy-like 元気がなくなるようにする　14 . . . was what I had reference to ～という話をした　18 round about 界隈の　24 ought to . . . ～すべきである

p.15　4 flower-pots 植木鉢　5 window-sill 窓台　17 Good Gracious! おやおや！　19 porridge（オートミールなどの）粥　23 What would have been the good? そんなことをして何の意味がある？

p.16　24 twitching ピクピク動かしている

p.17　9 altogether 完全に　13 pugs パグ（犬種）　16 plow-horse 農耕馬　21 spavins 飛節内腫（馬の関節炎）　22 spectacles 眼鏡　22 going blind 失明しかけている

p.18　14 complain 文句を言う　20 potato-bug コロラドハムシ（ジャガイモにつく害虫）　21 mustard-plaster からし軟膏

p.19　1 as a rule いつもは　2 patient 寛大　2 don't make much fuss つまらないことで大騒ぎしない　5 booby ばか　5 monkey with . . . 〜にいたずらする

p.20　5 common sight ありふれた風景　6 farm-animals 家畜　13 cure 治療する　20 harvest-mice カヤネズミ　20 water-voles ミズハタネズミ　20 badgers アナグマ　20 bats コウモリ

p.21　5 cellar 地下貯蔵室

p.22　12 Presently 間もなく　24 wags his tail しっぽを振る

p.23　1 annoy いらいらさせる　1 dreadfully ものすごく　1 such airs they put on なんて気取っているんだろう　3 macaw コンゴウインコ　6 Greek ギリシャ語　9 couldn't stand . . . 〜が我慢できなかった　10 what's become of . . . ～はどうなったか　11 geography 地理学　12 Golly! まったく！　14 hedge-sparrow ヨーロッパカヤクグリ　14 never hear the end of . . . ～について何度も聞かされる　22 King Charles was still hiding in the oak-tree チャールズ国王はまだオークの木に隠れていた（イングランド・スコットランド皇太子チャールズ、後のチャールズ2世は、1651年のウスターの戦いに敗れたあと敵から逃れるためにオークの木に身を隠して助かったとされる）

The Third Chapter
MORE MONEY TROUBLES

p.24　10 never had the heart to . . . ～する勇気がなかった　16 organ-grinder 手回しオルガン奏者

p.25　4 shilling シリング（1971年以前の英国の通貨単位）　10 rude 失礼な

p.26　2 toothache 歯痛　17 lap-dogs ペット用小型犬

p.27　3 be well off 裕福である　3 be ruined entirely 完全に破滅する　4 the last straw 我慢の限度を超えさせるもの　10 nasty 不快な　16 minds his own business いらぬおせっかいをしない　17 well behaved 行儀の良い　17 fussy 細かいことにこだわる　19 linoleum リノリウム（床仕上げ材の一種）

p. 28　2 mouths to fill 食べ物を与えなければならない者たち　4 mending 修繕、繕い物　5 butcher's bill 肉屋の勘定　7 nuisance 面倒

p.29 5 arithmetic 算数 10 for our sakes 私たちのために 16 dust ほこりを払う 16 make the beds ベッドを整える 17 keep the accounts 帳簿をつける 19 laundress 洗濯を仕事とする女性

p.30 2 tidy 整然とした 6 stall 露店

p.31 6 fishmonger 魚屋 8 hens lay eggs 雌鶏が卵を産む 9 junket 凝乳（牛乳を凝固させた甘い食べ物） 16 hauled 運んだ

The Fourth Chapter

A MESSAGE FROM AFRICA

p.32 11 out of breath 息を切らして

p.33 5 swallow ツバメ 6 rain-butt 天水桶 8 perished とても寒い 10 huddled 身を丸くしている 11 shivering 震えている 13 mantelpiece 炉棚 16 bitter weather 悪天候 23 twopence 2ペンス銅貨 26 rattle がらがら(おもちゃ)

p.34 1 teething 歯が生えている 7 measles はしか

p.35 5 dormice ヤマネ（山鼠） 16 pilot-bread 堅パン 17 hard tack 堅パン 18 anchor 錨

p.36 9 grocer 食料雑貨商 18 stable 馬小屋 24 suet-pudding スエットプディング（牛や羊の腎臓の周りの脂肪で作るプディング）

p.37 13 bunk 寝台

The Fifth Chapter
THE GREAT JOURNEY

p.40 7 shooting star 流れ星 11 no end とても

p.41 10 last longer 長持ちする 11 Equator 赤道 21 school of porpoises ネズミイルカの群れ

p.42 15 sure enough 案の定 21 torrents 滝のように 24 rolled over on its side 横転した

p.43 2 ship-wrecked 難破した 20 life-line 命綱

p.44 3 timbers 材木 5 took shelter 避難した 5 cave 洞窟

p.45 22 relatives 親戚 26 exhausted 疲れ果てた

p.46 3 be drowned 溺れる 8 stowaway 密航者 25 strangers よそ者

The Sixth Chapter
POLYNESIA AND THE KING

p.49 2 thick forest 深い森

p.50 3 ivory tusks 象牙質の牙 4 without so much as . . . ～もせずに 9 Medicine-Man 呪医 12 dungeon 地下牢 21 dim 薄暗い

p.51 3 just like her いかにも彼女らしい 3 Sneaked off こっそり姿を消した 13 ruse 策略 14 beak くちばし 18 creep through こっそり通り抜ける

p.52 12 peeped in 中をのぞいた 17 coughed 咳をした 18 mimic まねる

p.54 3 How dare you . . . よくも～できたな　13 invisible 目に見えない　21 mumps おたふく風邪

p.55 7 latchkey 掛け金の鍵

The Seventh Chapter

THE BRIDGE OF APES

p.56 3 gnashed his teeth 歯ぎしりした　3 rage 激怒　8 servants 使用人　9 tutor 家庭教師

p.57 6 strange land 未知の土地　6 not know his way 地理に明るくない　13 hollow tree 中が空洞になっている木

p.58 8 cocoanuts ココナッツ　14 dates ナツメヤシの実　14 figs イチジク　14 ground-nuts ピーナッツ

p.59 18 Noah and the Flood ノアの洪水　20 mutton 羊肉　25 nibbling 少しずつかじる

p.60 2 scurry round あわてて走り回る　23 swamp 沼

p.61 11 hastened on 先を急いだ

p.63 1 caught fast 引っかかった　8 steep cliff 険しい崖　13 Golly! 何てこった！　23 loose 放たれた　24 Get lively! キビキビやれ！　26 gazed 見つめた

p.64 6 his back was turned 背を向けていた　6 quick as a flash あっという間に　12 dizzy height 目もくらむ高い所　24 explorers 探検家　25 naturalists 博物学者　25 lain long weeks hidden 何週間も隠れていた

p.65 2 Bridge of Apes 猿の橋

The Eighth Chapter

THE LEADER OF THE LIONS

p.66 4 baboons ヒヒ　4 marmosets マーモセット、キヌザル　10 be vaccinated 予防接種を受ける

p.68 5 nursing 看護　7 antelopes レイヨウ　9 proud creature 誇り高い生き物　11 scornful 軽蔑に満ちた　12 glaring にらみつけて　14 King of Beasts 百獣の王　14 wait on . . . 〜に仕える

p.70 2 turning up his nose 鼻であしらって　3 stalked away 怒って出ていった　7 timid 気が小さい　8 pawed 前脚でかいた　11 frantic 取り乱した　16 den 巣穴　19 cubs（クマなどの肉食獣の）子　26 cunning 狡猾な

p.71 2 poorly 具合が悪い　5 drove him out 追い出した　6 You never did have a grain of sense! あなたは昔からひとかけらの分別もなかった！　13 offend 怒らせる　24 not fit to be . . . 〜になる資格がない

p.72 11 oblige . . . 〜の喜ぶことをする　14 do their share 役目を果たす　17 anxious 心配して　23 plains 平原

p.73 7 without even turning over 寝返りも打たずに

The Ninth Chapter

THE MONKEYS' COUNCIL

p.74 council 議会

p.75 14 owes money 借金をしている

p.76 13 paltry つまらない

p.77 4 grateful 感謝している 13 bunches of bananas 房のバナナ 22 menageries 動物園

p.78 4 easily amused つまらないことで喜ぶ

The Tenth Chapter

THE RAREST ANIMAL OF ALL

p.79 1 extinct 絶滅した 7 horns 角（つの）

p.80 1 huntsmen 猟師 10 peculiar 奇妙な 21 it was no use . . . ～しても無駄だ

p.81 13 persuade 説得する

p.82 3 make up its mind 心を決める 9 your fortune's made 一財産築ける 14 pinch and scrape けちけちして節約する 20 be sensible 分別を失うな

p.84 8 I am the only one who will do. 目的を果たせるのは私だけだ。 15 Chamois シャモア（レイヨウの一種）

p.86 4 for all time 永遠に 4 mark the spot 目印をつける 5 heart of . . . ～の中心

The Eleventh Chapter

THE BLACK PRINCE

p.87 8 tread softly そっと歩く　8 talk low 小声で話す

p.88 1 Never lift your foot till you come to the stile. 踏み段のところに行くまで足を上げるな（取り越し苦労をするな）。　17 lost their way 道に迷った　18 strayed a long way off the path 道から大きくそれた　19 creepers and vines つる植物　22 stumbled into 偶然入り込んだ　23 boggy ぬかるんでいる　24 convolvulus-runners セイヨウヒルガオのつる　25 thorns とげ　26 underbrush やぶ

p.89 2 come upon . . . ～を見つける　3 blundering about うろうろ歩き回って　15 scrub 磨く　25 hinges 蝶番

p.90 11 put things right 事態を収拾する

p.91 12 gravel-walk 砂利道　20 weary 疲れた　21 spots ニキビ　25 thee そなた　26 perchance もしかすると

p.92 1 started up 跳び上がった　3 Methought 私は思った　5 yonder あそこの　5 bower 木陰　7 thou sayest そなたは言う　10 rose-bud バラのつぼみ　12 clasping his hands 両手を握り締めて　17 mighty deeds とてつもない偉業　18 languishing 苦しんでいる　19 lingering 延々と続く　20 behold 見よ！　22 fair lady 美しい女性

The Twelfth Chapter

MEDICINE AND MAGIC

p.94 14 get rid of . . . ～を取り除く 14 pimples ニキビ

p.95 3 in the blink of an eye あっという間に 5 re-dyed 染め直した 5 Shall the leopard change his spots, or the Ethiopian his skin ひょうはその斑点を、エチオピヤびとはその皮膚を変えることができようか（聖書の言葉から） 8 impatiently いらいらして 16 liberated chlorine 遊離塩素 17 pigment 色素 18 zinc-ointment 亜鉛華軟膏 18 temporary measure 一時的な措置 23 The Sleeping Beauty『眠れる森の美女』 26 shining armor 輝くよろい 26 gauntlets（中世の騎士が用いたよろいの）こて

p.96 3 'Tis「it is」の短縮形 10 potions 水薬

p.97 20 basin 洗面器 26 fidgety 落ち着きのない

p.98 10 looking-glass 鏡 22 undid はずした

p.99 22 waggling her tail 小刻みに尻尾を振って 23 Serve him right 自業自得だ

p.100 13 handsome is as handsome does 行ないの立派なのが立派な人 14 booby まぬけ 17 taking a snooze うたた寝をして 19 Silly business! ばかばかしい！

p.101 5 lonesome さびしい 22 swarm 群れ

p.102 5 skimming すれすれに飛んで 9 rustling さらさらいう音 10 settle on . . . ～に降り立つ 24 set the sail 帆を揚げろ

The Thirteenth Chapter
RED SAILS AND BLUE WINGS

p.104 1 homeward 家路へ向かって 14 mischief わるさ

p.105 16 underdone 生焼けの

p.106 10 scoundrels 悪党 19 swift 速い 24 fetch 取ってくる

p.107 19 soup-tureen スープを入れる深皿 20 barge 平底の荷船

p.108 3 unravel ほぐす

The Fourteenth Chapter
THE RATS' WARNING

p.109 3 short of breath 息切れして

p.110 1 romp はね回る 17 leave a sinking ship 沈む船からいなくなる 21 sneer 冷笑 21 disgraceful 恥ずかしい

p.111 6 rotten 腐っている

p.112 3 tingly ちくちくする 4 foot's asleep 足がしびれている 9 piebald（白黒）まだらの 11 jaundice 黄疸 21 considerate 思いやりがある 26 pails バケツ 26 saucepans 片手鍋

p.113 17 meadows 草地 18 bird-seed 小鳥が食べる種子類 23 squeaked キーキー声で鳴いた 25 sugar-cane サトウキビ

p.114 3 flustered 慌てふためいて

The Fifteenth Chapter

THE BARBARY DRAGON

p.115 2 cold in his head 鼻風邪　3 damp 湿った　7 sneezed くしゃみをした　23 open sea 外海

p.116 12 Be pleasant to . . . ～に感じよく接する　13 bound to . . . ～する運命にある　22 rascals 悪党

p.117 6 glee 歓喜

p.118 1 bad names 悪口　5 cracking jokes 冗談を言っている　5 puzzled 戸惑った　6 uneasy 不安な　8 bellowed out 怒鳴るように叫んだ　9 leaking 水漏れしている　10 peered じっと見た　16 duffers 愚か者　23 standing on its head 逆立ちしている　24 cling しがみつく

p.119 2 plunged 突っ込んだ　3 gurgling sound ゴボゴボという音　4 bobbing ぷかぷか浮かんで　19 poking his nose out of the water 鼻を水から突き出して

p.120 4 attentive 思いやりがある　15 'twould「it would」の短縮形　16 if the seas were rid of you おまえが海からいなくなったら　24 give up being a pirate 海賊であることをやめる

p.121 5 turned pale 青ざめた　6 groaned うめいた　6 in disgust 不快そうに　9 stout 頑丈な　23 punish 罰する　24 so long as . . . ～である限りは

The Sixteenth Chapter

TOO-TOO, THE LISTENER

p.123 2 set off 出発した　10 dusk 夕暮れ

p.124　2 primrose 淡緑黄色　6 larder 食糧貯蔵室

p.125　2 Kashmir カシミヤ　3 cobweb クモの巣　3 embroidered 刺繍をした　8 coral サンゴ　8 amber 琥珀　12 mother o' pearl（真珠貝などの）真珠層　16 stood against the wall 壁に立てかけてあった

p.126　13 good hearers 耳がいい者たち

p.127　20 hold your breath 息を止めて　22 pesky やっかいな

p.128　2 blubber 泣きじゃくる　2 sniffle 鼻をすする　3 lest . . . ～しないように　8 Pshaw! ふん！　8 ignorance 無知

The Seventeenth Chapter

THE OCEAN GOSSIPS

p.129　gossips うわさ好きな人たち　3 clamber through よじ登る　5 struck a match マッチを擦った　9 fastened しっかり留めた　11 pewter しろめ製の　13 winey ワインのような　15 rum room ラム酒の部屋

p.130　2 giddy 目まいがする

p.132　13 gets so dreadfully embarrassed ひどく恥ずかしがる

p.133　3 Saucy 生意気な　3 cutter-rigged カッター型帆装の　4 sloop スループ型帆船(1本マストに縦帆の帆装を持つ)

p.134　5 nephew 甥　12 Decapods 十脚類（エビ、カニなどの甲殻類）　13 shell-fish 貝類

The Eighteenth Chapter
SMELLS

p.135 13 Black Eagle カザノワシ　14 Bald Eagle ハクトウワシ　14 Fish Eagle ウミワシ　14 Golden Eagle イヌワシ　15 Eagle-Vulture ヤシハゲワシ　15 White-tailed Sea Eagle オジロワシ

p.136 2 round-shouldered 猫背の　3 stern いかめしい　3 gleaming きらめく　4 shot darting glances さっとあちこちに視線を向けた　22 parted company 別々の道を進んだ

p.137 2 scorch 焦がす　10 wheelbarrow 手押し車　22 no two ways about that ほかの考えはない　23 lad 少年

p.138 9 conceited うぬぼれている

p.140 11 Snuff 嗅ぎたばこ　11 by Jingo! まったく！　11 Black Rappee ブラック・ラペー（嗅ぎたばこの銘柄）　16 as good as found 見つかったも同じだ　17 'Twill「it will」の短縮形

p.141 17 muttering つぶやいて　18 Tar（たばこの）タール、やに　18 kerosene 灯油　19 laurel-leaves 月桂樹の葉

p.142 1 mongrel 雑種犬　4 dainty 上品な　16 lead 鉛　16 dove-cote ハト小屋　17 granary 穀物倉　18 kid gloves 山羊皮の手袋　20 drinking-trough 水を入れる飼い葉桶　20 sycamores アメリカスズカケノキ　23 parsnips アメリカボウフウ

p.143 4 fake 偽物　22 Enough is as good as a feast 満腹はご

ちそうも同様（諺）

The Nineteenth Chapter

THE ROCK

p.145 **5** mist 薄い霧、靄　**6** fog 霧　**10** frightfully 恐ろしく　**17** rudder 舵　**17** steer 操舵する

p.147 **8** starving 飢えている　**26** harnessed 引き具でつなげた

p.148 **1** bounding はずんで　**5** tremendously 猛烈に　**12** chattering おしゃべり　**18** perched 止まった　**18** startled 驚かせた

p.149 **7** screwed up their eyes 目を細めた　**11** gull カモメ　**11** star-fish ヒトデ　**11** shred 切れ端　**11** seaweed 海藻　**13** straining their ears 耳を凝らして　**15** gentle lapping of the little waves ひたひたと洗う波

p.150 **10** close at his heels すぐ後ろから

p.151 **5** fast asleep 熟睡して

The Twentieth Chapter

THE FISHERMAN'S TOWN

p.153 **21** Hark to . . . ～を聞け　**21** gale 強風

p.154 **20** giggled and blushed くすくす笑い、顔を赤らめた

p.155 **15** wicked 危険な

p.156 **2** Mayor of the town 町長　**8** page boys 小姓　**15** token（感謝の）しるし　**22** parcel 包み

p.157　**1** admiration and respect 称賛と尊敬の念

The Last Chapter
HOME AGAIN

p.158　**9** country-fairs 郡主催の品評会　**10** Punch-and-Judy show パンチとジュディというキャラクターが登場する人形劇

p.159　**21** longing to . . . ～したいと強く願っている　**23** came flocking 群がってきた

p.161　**1** hollyhocks タチアオイ　**7** under the eaves 軒下　**17** horseradish セイヨウワサビ　**26** drafty すきま風が通る

（後註執筆・星野真理／翻訳家）

KODANSHA ENGLISH LIBRARY

ドリトル先生《せんせい》アフリカ行《ゆ》き

The Story of Doctor Dolittle

2020年11月10日　第1刷発行

著　者　ヒュー・ロフティング
発行者　渡瀬昌彦
発行所　株式会社講談社
〒112-8001　東京都文京区音羽2-12-21
販売　東京03-5395-3606
業務　東京03-5395-3615
編　集　株式会社講談社エディトリアル
代表　堺 公江
〒112-0013　東京都文京区音羽1-17-18 護国寺SIAビル
編集部　東京03-5319-2171
本文DTP　ギルド
印刷・製本所　大日本印刷株式会社

2020 Printed in Japan
ISBN 978-4-06-513326-2

まんが日本昔話③

Once Upon a Time in Japan 3

「金太郎」「かぐや姫」「うばすて山」「舌切り雀」「浦島太郎」など、全 10 編収録。

銀河鉄道の夜　宮沢賢治

Night Train to the Stars

ジョバンニとカムパネラがめぐる一夜限りの空の旅。その終着点にあったのは……。

注文の多い料理店　宮沢賢治

Restaurant of Many Orders

表題作のほか、「なめとこ山の熊」「よだかの星」など 7 つの短編を収録。

イソップ物語　イソップ

Aesop's Fables

「北風と太陽」「すっぱいぶどう」「狼が来た」など、おなじみの 40 話。

ふしぎの国のアリス　ルイス・キャロル

Alice's Adventures in Wonderland

チョッキを着たウサギを追って穴に飛び込んでしまったアリス。たどりついた先は奇想天外なところで……！

鏡の国のアリス　ルイス・キャロル

Through the Looking-Glass

暖炉の上の鏡を通り抜け、鏡の国に入り込んだアリス。ハンプティ・ダンプティなどおかしな住人が次々と現れ……。

チーズバーガーズ　ボブ・グリーン

Cheeseburgers

「80 年代アメリカのスナップ写真」と著者が称する多数のコラムの中から 27 編を厳選。

アメリカン・ビート　ボブ・グリーン
American Beat

アメリカを代表する人気コラムニストが描き出す、素顔のアメリカ。コラム 26 編を収録。

クリスマス・キャロル　チャールズ・ディケンズ
Christmas Carol

12 月 24 日の夜、強欲でひねくれた老人の元に幽霊が現れ……。クリスマスに読むべき一冊。

ティファニーで朝食を　トルーマン・カポーティ
Breakfast at Tiffany's

ニューヨークを舞台に、奔放な愛に生きるホリーの姿を描き出したカポーティの傑作。

ライ麦畑でつかまえて　J・D・サリンジャー
The Catcher in the Rye

思春期特有の少年の心理を見事に描き上げた、サリンジャーの世界的ベストセラー。

ナイン・ストーリーズ　J・D・サリンジャー
Nine Stories

「バナナフィッシュ日和」「笑い男」「テディ」など、サリンジャーの自選短編集。

老人と海　アーネスト・ヘミングウェイ
The Old Man and the Sea

老漁夫と巨大なカジキマグロの死闘を描いた、20 世紀文学を代表する傑作。

オズの魔法使い　L・フランク・バウム
The Wizard of Oz
たつまきに巻き込まれて別世界に運ばれたドロシー。犬のトトたちを連れた冒険が始まる！

グリム童話集　グリム兄弟
Grimm's Fairy Tales
「白雪姫」「ヘンゼルとグレーテル」「ブレーメンの音楽師たち」など10話を収録。

O・ヘンリー短編集　O・ヘンリー
The Gift of the Magi
「賢者の贈り物」「最後の一葉」「警官と賛美歌」など、主にニューヨークを舞台にした9編を収録。

シャーロック・ホームズの冒険　コナン・ドイル
The Adventures of Sherlock Holmes
「赤毛クラブ」「まだらのひも」「唇のねじれた男」「ブナの木屋敷」の4編で構成された一冊。

華麗なるギャツビー　フィッツジェラルド
The Great Gatsby
謎に包まれた男ギャツビー。その華麗なる生活に隠されたものとは。映画の原作本。

アガサ・クリスティ短編集　アガサ・クリスティ
Agatha Christie's Best Stories
クリスティが生んだ名探偵、ミス・マープルとエルキュール・ポアロが短編集で「共演」！

美女と野獣　ボーモン夫人
Beauty and the Beast
ミュージカルや映画にもなって大ヒットした作品の原作。わかりやすい英語にリライト。

クマのプーさん　A・A・ミルン
Winnie-The-Pooh
世界中で愛されているクマのプーさん。E・H・シェパードの挿絵とともに楽しめる一冊。

たのしいムーミン一家　トーベ・ヤンソン
Finn Family Moomintroll
おなじみのムーミン谷の仲間たちが繰り広げる、ユーモラスな傑作ファンタジー。

ムーミン谷の彗星　トーベ・ヤンソン
Comet in Moominland
ムーミン谷に、真っ赤に燃える彗星がどんどん近づいてくる！　皆の運命はいかに……？

エルマーのぼうけん　ルース・スタイルス・ガネット
My Father's Dragon
拾ったノラ猫の話を聞いたエルマーは、竜を探しに南の島へ。不思議な冒険が始まった。

ライオンと魔女　C・S・ルイス
The Lion, the Witch, and the Wardrobe
ナルニア国に迷い込んだルーシィたち４人兄弟。そこでは白い魔女との戦いが待っていた！　ファンタジーの名作。

五体不満足　完全版　乙武洋匡

No One's Perfect

500 万部を超える大ベストセラーの英語版。各国で感動を巻き起こした。

星の王子さま　サン=テクジュペリ

The Little Prince

砂漠に不時着した飛行士がめぐりあった、星の王子さま。子どもも大人も心打たれる不朽の名作。

チョコレート工場の秘密　ロアルド・ダール

Charlie and the Chocolate Factory

ワンカ氏の世界一大きなチョコレート工場の見学に招かれたチャーリーら5 人の子どもたち。そこでの驚くべき体験とは？！

モリー先生との火曜日　ミッチ・アルボム

Tuesdays with Morrie

卒業後 16 年ぶりに再会した恩師は難病 ALS に侵されていた。2 人だけの火曜日の授業が始まった。

アルケミスト　パウロ・コエーリョ

The Alchemist

羊飼いをしていた少年は夢のお告げに従って宝物を探す旅に出た。勇気と感動を与える名著。

十二番目の天使　オグ・マンディーノ

The Twelfth Angel

ビジネスで大成功したジョンだったが、事故で妻と息子を失ってしまう。ある時、息子に瓜二つの少年と出会い……。

きみに読む物語　ニコラス・スパークス

The Notebook

病身のノアと記憶をなくした妻のアリー。2人の愛の軌跡とそれを綴ったノートをめぐる物語。

かもめのジョナサン　リチャード・バック

Jonathan Livingston Seagull

群れを追放された一羽のかもめ。その生き方を通して、自由な精神を貫くことの大切さを描き出す。

動物農場　ジョージ・オーウェル

Animal Farm

理想を掲げて起こした反乱が、やがて旧体制を上回る独裁制に変貌する様を寓話風に描いたオーウェルの傑作。

十五少年漂流記　ジュール・ベルヌ

A Two Years' Vacation

嵐のせいで無人島へ漂着した15人の少年。力を合わせ、島で生き抜こうとするのだったが……。

思い出のマーニー　ジョーン・G・ロビンソン

When Marnie was There

英国の風景と思春期の少女の成長を美しい筆致で描いた、隠れた名作。スタジオジブリ映画化作品。

スター・ウォーズ　エピソード4／新たなる希望

ジョージ・ルーカス／ライダー・ウィンダム

STAR WARS: Episode IV—A New Hope

壮大なスケールで繰り広げられる傑作SF大作。スター・ウォーズはこの作品から始まった！

ジャングル・ブック　ラドヤード・キプリング
The Jungle Book
インドのジャングルに取り残され、オオカミに育てれた人間の子ども、モウグリの冒険譚。

そして誰もいなくなった　アガサ・クリスティ
And Then There Were None
謎の人物によって孤島に集められた男女10人。童謡の歌詞のとおりに1人また1人と殺されていき……。

ルドルフとイッパイアッテナ　斉藤洋
Rudolf and Ippai Attena
間違って東京に来てしまった黒猫のルドルフ。ノラ猫たちの友情と冒険を描いた児童文学の名著。

オリエント急行殺人事件　アガサ・クリスティ
Murder on the Orient Express
ヨーロッパを走る豪華列車の中でアメリカ人の富豪が刺殺された。ポアロは事件解決に挑むが、乗客にはすべて完璧なアリバイがあった！

人魚姫　アンデルセン童話集　ハンス・クリスチャン・アンデルセン
The Little Mermaid and Other Stories
表題作のほか、「マッチ売りの少女」「醜いアヒルの子」「裸の王様」など9編を収録。

…話題作、続刊予定！

講談社バイリンガル・コミックス シリーズ　好評既刊

対訳よりぬきコボちゃん　植田まさし

KOBO, the Li'l Rascal

コボちゃんの可愛らしさが凝縮された一冊。4コマ漫画だから英語もわかりやすい。

バイリンガル版

あさきゆめみし　星の章　大和和紀

The Tale of Genji: Stars

美しき永遠のラブストーリー。読むだけで源氏物語がよくわかる一冊。

バイリンガル版

あさきゆめみし　花の章　大和和紀

The Tale of Genji: Flowers

愛する人は数知れず。そんな源氏をとりまく主要人物系図も収録。

バイリンガル版

ちはやふる①、②、③　末次由紀

Chihayafuru

大人気シリーズの最初の部分をバイリンガル化。特別付録として巻末に百人一首の英訳と現代語訳つき（1巻には第一首から第五十首までを、2巻には第五十一首から第百首までを収録）。

バイリンガル版

のだめカンタービレ①、②、③　二ノ宮知子

Nodame Cantabile

好き勝手にピアノを弾くのだめと、のだめに愛されるエリート音大生千秋が贈るドタバタコメディ。第1巻はLesson 1からLesson 9までを、第2巻はLesson 10からLesson 18までを、第3巻はLesson 19からLesson 27を収録。
